GIRL GEEK

A Gaming The System Novel

Brenna Aubrey

SILVER GRIFFON ASSOCIATES
ORANGE, CA, USA

Silver Griffon Associates
P.O. Box 7383
Orange, CA 92863

Publisher's Note: This is a work of fiction. Names, characters, places, and incidents are a product of the author's imagination. Locales and public names are sometimes used for atmospheric purposes. Any resemblance to actual people, living or dead, or to businesses, companies, events, institutions, or locales is completely coincidental.

Trademarked names appear throughout this book. Rather than use a trademark symbol with every occurrence of a trademarked name, names are used in an editorial fashion, with no intention of infringement of the respective owner's trademark.

Book Layout ©2017 BookDesignTemplates.com
Cover Art ©2019 Julianne Burke, Heart to Cover, LLC

Girl Geek / Brenna Aubrey. – 1st ed.
First Printing 2017
Printed in the USA
ISBN 978-1-940951-41-6

This one is for the awesome members of the Brenna Aubrey Book Group on Facebook. For all the fun times we have together and for your love of this story in particular.

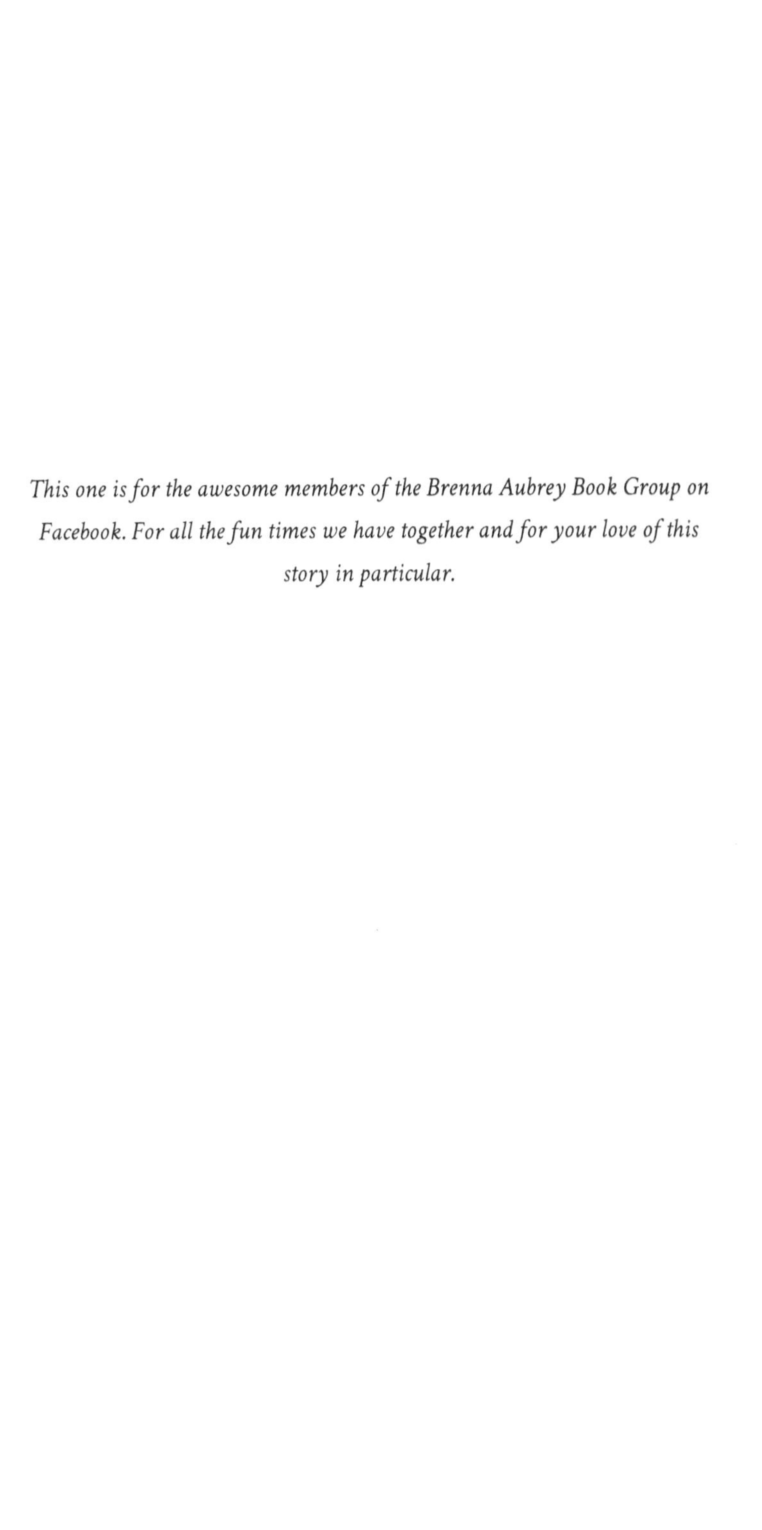

This one is for the awesome members of the Brenna Aubrey Book Group on Facebook. For all the fun times we have together and for your love of this story in particular.

Please advise. And, while you're at it, get some game designers who have normal, healthy sex lives—or even, OMG!, hire a female—so they'll be less inclined to display their fantasies on the screen (unless more of those fantasies coincide with mine). Muchas gracias and merci beaucoup!

Well, folks, you heard it here first. Girl Geek will be beta-testing the new game, Dragon Epoch, and I will report back ASAP. I'm getting my hands dirty so you don't have to—and never fear, ladies, I'm taking no prisoners (unless the game calls for it, of course!).

Chapter 1:
A Whole New World

I SKIMMED THE NON-DISCLOSURE AGREEMENT, NOTING ANY possible loopholes that would allow me to write about the game. As far as NDAs go, this one was short and to the point...

Non-disclosure, shmon-disclosure. Beta-testers always had to agree to one, but I was sure I could cleverly skirt the letter of the law enough to intrigue my readers. Okay, so it forbade me from discussing game mechanics, in-game items, or divulging details about quests. *Details, details.*

After electronically signing and submitting the document, I reread the last bit of my most recent blog post, made a few tweaks and then hit "post" on my blog. It wasn't easy producing new daily content, but it was paying off. My readership was increasing by the day—even more so since I'd started blogging about Dragon Epoch.

I wasn't the *only* person out there excited about this game!

My gaze lit on my textbook sitting neglected on the far side of my desk. All this blogging about gaming wasn't interfering with my schoolwork—*yet.* But the new game, on top of the hospital job I'd just started last month, worried me. What time dilation effect would Dragon Epoch have? Would it suck hours of my life away in the blink of an eye? *Danger, Will Robinson!*

Good thing I had no social life whatsoever. I did have acquaintances from a pre-med student study group, but when we were together, we talked medical terminology, commiserated over the impending MCAT, and strategized about how best to pad our résumés for med school.

Right after posting to the blog, my computer screen flipped out—lines and waves covered the screen. I reached over and thumped the blocky monitor on its side. *Damn it!* It couldn't break now. Not with this delicious new game on the horizon.

And now that my blog revenue was increasing—apparently, regular content will do that—this was like a second job. It *could* pay off. Someday. Though I suspected that if I sat down and calculated how much I actually made, it would end up paying pennies per hour. Not much less than the nurse's assistant job, in point of fact.

But I did it for my love of writing and chatting about my favorite hobby—gaming!

At least the blogging was fun. For now. I'd work on a plan for later.

Just as I was pounding on my keyboard, the front door opened and slammed a second later. My roomie entered in time to witness the end of my temper tantrum. His eyes narrowed as he took in the scene.

"What's good, Mia?" He threw his backpack onto the couch—from where *I'd* have to remove it in a few hours, most likely. My roommate, Heath Bowman, was not the tidiest of people. In truth, he was a slob. But as he was also my brother-from-another-mother, I tolerated it. And just as any good sister would do, I bitched at him about it. Often.

"You need a new monitor," he said. "Hell, you need a completely new box, but that's beside the point."

"Wow, that's some amazing deduction work, Sherlock." I leaned back in my chair, folding my arms across my chest and gave him the once-over. Heath was as tall, powerfully built and blond as an ancient Viking. A handsome guy—though I had never thought about him in *that* way. Good thing, since he also happened to be as gay as I was straight. "What do you do for an encore, shit your pants?"

His brows rose. "Aren't you a grouchy one today?"

I rubbed at the crick in the back of my neck. "I didn't sleep very well last night, and I fell asleep in my Lit class this morning. The teacher called me out. It was embarrassing."

He frowned. "What's with this sudden bout of insomnia? That's like the third time in the last two weeks."

I shrugged. "I have no idea. Just MCAT nerves, I guess." Yeah, the dreaded MCAT... I was trying to play it cool. Trying to get in a minimum of an hour of study time every day, but as the test date approached, my anxiety seemed to be creeping up the angst scale.

Meditation. I needed to take up meditation in my copious amounts of spare time. Since *medication* didn't seem to be a viable option, anyway.

"You're stressing out over nothing. You have months to get ready for it. And you learn by osmosis."

I quirked my mouth. "Jealous."

He shrugged. Heath had never been one for school. Especially tests. Which is why he'd gone to community college—and finished up already—while I attended the neighboring university, Chapman. After that, he'd landed himself a nice job in web design. One that often allowed him to work from home.

Heath nodded at my troublesome computer monitor. "I just got a bonus for finishing a redesign on that Harrison and Sons website a month early. I'm going to use it to buy myself a kickass new monitor and video card, so I can enjoy Dragon Epoch in all its glory. I'll give you my old one. Besides, no one uses those clunky CRT things anymore. They're shitty and they take up way too much room. That computer is straight out of the Jurassic era."

I popped out of my seat and hooked my arms around his neck, kissing him on the cheek. He made the requisite sour lemon face, as per usual and also expected. Heath, my dear friend, never changed. And hadn't changed much in the almost-decade that I'd known him.

"You rock, my friend. Thank you."

"Well, when you're a rich and famous doctor, you can pay me back."

I grinned. "I most certainly will. Free medical advice for life."

He rolled his eyes. "Greaaaaat..." And with that, he disappeared into his room. The backpack, of course, was left behind and forgotten until I accidentally sat on it hours later.

Yep indeed. He never changed....

For example, he always kept his promises, which meant that, only days later, Heath brought home his new monitor. And just as quickly, he pulled my box apart to get the clunky old thing to work right.

"Christ, I feel like I'm at an archeological dig," he huffed, rearranging the cards within. He picked up the can of compressed air and began blowing into the innards of—okay, I'd begrudgingly admit—my ancient box. When he blew the cold air into the box, huge clouds of dust rose everywhere.

Heath's boyfriend, Brian, sat nearby and made a big show of waving his hand in front of his face and coughing. "Jeez. Someone needs to learn how to do housework better," he chided while sending me a snotty look.

Though I felt the heat rise in my cheeks and forehead—*scathing* heat, as a matter of fact—I did what I always did and bit my tongue.

Were that expression literal instead of figurative, I would have bitten it in half by now!

"Everybody's box gets dusty," Heath retorted in my defense. "The archeological dig comment was about the ancient technology. Straight out of the Atlantean civilization of *Stargate*. I half expect it to open up a wormhole into another world."

To emphasize the difference in my tolerance of Heath's teasing over Brian's snark, I laughed. "You love a challenge. Always have."

"*Always have,*" Brian repeated with exaggerated air quotes and a nasty tone of voice. "You haven't known each other long enough to make a statement like that."

I chewed my lip. "I think knowing one another half our lives qualifies."

Brian frowned. "That math is wrong."

My face again burned. Heath, who had been buried in his task—or so I'd thought—looked up from his work. "What does it even matter?" he snapped.

Brian didn't reply, only shrugged and rolled his eyes. He stood from where he'd been sitting on the arm of the couch and snatched up his book bag. "I've got to get going. See you."

Heath stiffened when Brian headed straight to the door and left without a goodbye kiss or any kind words.

My brows shot up but I said nothing, and in minutes, Heath was back to work. I frowned as I watched him, wondering what was up with those two. Dare I bring up how much I disliked Brian's general treatment of him?

Teeth marks on my tongue. That's what I was going to get...

After ten more minutes, he straightened, dramatically wiping his brow with the back of his hand. "There you go... a miracle exhibition of my finest skills in Computer Paleontology."

I clapped my hands together, excited. "Thank you!" He acknowledged my gratitude with a curt nod, obviously distracted. Perhaps thinking of Brian's display of rudeness earlier. I cleared my throat. "So... we're logging on to the new beta tonight, right?" I asked, an eyebrow arched.

Heath glanced at me out of the corner of his eye before pushing up and heading into the kitchen. From the smell of it, he'd brewed a new pot of coffee. I frowned, following him. Something was definitely up, easily visible from the tension in his shoulders and his stiff stance.

"Are you two not getting along?" I asked quietly.

He let out a long breath and shrugged, but kept his back to me as he continued to fix his cup of coffee.

More silence between us. I leaned back against the counter and folded my arms across my chest, trying to resist the urge to bash on the little twerp. Brian seemed to enjoy yanking my best friend around, and that just brought out the protective she-bear in me.

They'd been dating for about six months, and it had been rocky from the start. But as Brian was Heath's first steady boyfriend after a long string of flings, I'd been thrilled for him… at first. Then I'd steadily had my doubts pile up with every diva-like demand that Brian put on Heath. They fought—a lot—but Heath was in love and determined to make it work.

I hated—*hated*—seeing my friend hurt. "What about this time?" I asked.

Heath shrugged, turning to face me. "He wants a bigger commitment."

I let out a breath. "You've been seeing each other exclusively for *months*. What else could he want? Marriage?"

He gritted his teeth but did not reply.

I snorted. Maybe that *was* it. "Go for it, but you're on your own, buddy. I'm *never* getting married."

He held the pitcher of coffee up as if to ask me if I wanted any. I shook my head. "So you've said. You're going to be a nun without the religion part of it."

I made a face but didn't say anything, waiting for him to answer the question. He ran a hand through his dark blond hair and sighed before responding.

"He wants us to live together."

I waited a beat for him to continue. Two beats. We locked gazes. I shrugged. "Why don't you invite him to move in, then?"

"Alone. Just the two of us."

Another beat, this one awkward and thick. I looked away. *What should I say?* Obviously it was his right to live with Brian— alone—if he wanted.

My hands held my arms just above the elbows as my grip tightened. I tried not to give away how much this hurt, but I couldn't prevent myself from feeling it. I swallowed before speaking again. "Alrighty, then."

As he sipped at his cup, his stance grew even more tense, possibly with remembered conflict. "I told him no way. I'm not throwing you out on the street. He pitched a fit and claimed that you mean more to me than he does."

Well. That explained the extra dose of snark this afternoon.

I'd gotten the impression pretty quickly that Brian didn't like me. I never claimed to be the most likeable person ever, but his behavior had seemed more on par with jealousy. Which was ridiculous. Neither Heath nor I had siblings—except what we were to each other. Heath was one-hundred percent gay and would never have any interest in me besides friendship, and I was one-hundred percent okay with that. But Brian was jealous of any amount of time Heath spent with me rather than him. I quietly wondered if the guy had other interests or hobbies outside of dating Heath. Apparently not.

Though there was a heavy weight in my stomach and a faint sting of betrayal that Heath was even considering this, I sucked it up and let him off the hook.

"Well, you don't necessarily have to kick me out in the street, you know. I can find a place on my own if you want to share these digs with him."

He shook his head vigorously and set the coffee cup back down. "No. You would stay here. I was thinking about buying a condo anyway. I've got the money saved up, and housing prices aren't half bad right now."

I read between the lines: Brian had not approved of our apartment as a livable place. My shoulders slumped at the thought of living here without Heath. We'd lived together since our sophomore year in high school.

At the age of fifteen, he'd come out to his parents, and his dad threw him out of the house. My mom extended welcoming arms, and he became a permanent guest at the family B&B. After graduation, we both moved to Orange County, and he'd been my roommate for the past three years.

I tried not to sound as hopeless and hollow as I felt. "I couldn't afford to live here on my own, and I don't know who I could ask to move in. You stay and I'll find something. Maybe student housing close to the school."

Heath's lips pressed together so ferociously that they went white. "I really hate this."

So did I… but there was no way I was going to make him choose between his boyfriend and me.

"I'm not going to be the reason that you are having problems with Brian, all right? I'm cool with it. All I ask is that you give me a little time to find something." I tilted my head up at him, shifting my weight to lean against the counter. "Will he calm down if you tell him I'm looking and have a move-out date? Say one or two months from now?"

"No less than two months. And if you need more—"

I shook my head adamantly. "I won't need more. I'll be fine. Call him and let him know that we're working on it."

Heath nodded but didn't look happy. And though I hated seeing my best friend in a rocky relationship, I couldn't deny the certain amount of self-satisfaction I felt that, at the ripe old age of twenty-one, I had avoided the ins and outs of navigating romantic relationships. I'd learned the hard way at a very young age that dating was most certainly *not* for me!

Ugh. Time to change the subject.

"So about the beta for that new video game..." I said, waggling my eyebrows.

Heath grinned, visibly relieved. "Yeah? Looks badass, doesn't it? The artwork. That game trailer... Uber dragons. Dynamic quests. I think I've died and gone to nerd heaven. Or I soon will."

I concurred. "It looks like it could be addictive. Promise me that we'll log on tonight? I think my computer has the bare minimum specs to run this if I turn off all the fancy effects."

"*Barely, sir,*" he said, imitating Scotty's accent from Star Trek. "The processors canna handle any more, Captain!"

"Well, it's all I got. And since I'm your favorite kickass gamer girl—"

He grabbed the cup off the counter, sipping again. "You wouldn't even be hooked on video games if it weren't for me..."

"*Pusher,*" I said, poking a finger into his broad chest.

He smirked at me. 'Junkie. *I'm* not the one who spent twenty-four hours straight on Dragon Age. That was all *you*, dollface."

I sighed dreamily in fond memory of that beloved game. "Oh, Alistair..."

Heath put down his coffee cup and picked up his phone. With a deep breath, he started to, I assumed, text Brian. "Okay, it's a date. You and me, tonight. Brian will be appeased, and he's working tonight anyway."

"Mmm. Good to know," I said, turning to leave the kitchen. I managed to fight rolling my eyes over the hot mess that was *Brian* until my back was turned.

Barely, sir...

Chapter 2:
When Eloisa Met FallenOne

T HE EVENING BROUGHT THE LONG-AWAITED CHANCE to beta test the new Dragon Epoch game. Finally, an immersive game to play after months of marking time, replaying the old stuff. Despite the artwork, which included scantily-clad models painted as lithe elvish women with large, gravity-defying breasts, the game looked promising. So, I cracked my knuckles—figuratively—and sat down in front of the keyboard, ready to *pwn* this game.

"Wow, look at these graphics," Heath said from his desk as he studied the fantastical scenery on his brand new high-definition screen. I struggled not to be jealous of him since he'd acquired it, especially since I'd at least gotten his hand-me-down out of the deal—and without it, I wouldn't be seeing any graphics at all.

I turned back to my screen, awed by the artistic, colorful depictions of the fantasy landscape. Rugged, distant mountains, yellow meadows, gently trickling streams... lush forests. Even with the display options turned down so I could run the bare minimum graphics on my computer, it was breathtaking. I'd read that, as time progressed, the game would depict the transformation of the seasons. I looked forward to seeing that.

"Let's get this party started!" I said, once I was done with the character creation screen. I'd chosen an elven spiritual enchantress, with long flowing black hair and eyes a neon shade of violet. I named her Eloisa. Of course, the poor dear didn't have a scrap of decent cloth to dress herself in. Her ass cheeks were hanging out in the wind, fully exposed to the elements—and the male gaze, of course. Gritting my teeth together, I determined to get my girl some junk armor as quickly as possible.

"This old fart elfy dude wants me to pick flowers for him," Heath grumbled. "Stupid ass quest."

After exploring for a few minutes, we found ourselves outside the city wall. And indeed, Heath had discovered a quest from an aging elf man dressed in a strange military uniform accentuated by a kilt.

"Aww... how sweet!" I said. "He lost his one true love, and he wants to remember her by taking flowers to a shrine in her name. I think that's really romantic."

"What do you know about romance?" Heath asked. "The girl who never dates. Who never even goes out. Forget *girl geek*, you're the *girl hermit*."

I laughed. "Social lives are so overrated. Especially when you have a game like this to play at home with your bestie."

After the first hour of our newest addiction, I could tell it was only going to get better—our enjoyment—or worse—our addiction. Depended on how you looked at it.

General SylvanWood—the "old fart elfy dude"—thanked us for completing his quest. Then he summarily referred us to another Non-Player Character (NPC), who started yet another interesting quest chain. Each mission led us deeper and deeper down a virtual rabbit hole.

Yes, there was some grinding involved—what decent game wouldn't be complete without the requisite grunt work to level up? But mostly it was an immersive story, filled with beautiful graphics and intriguing details that begged to be investigated.

This game was like crack—or worse, meth. And we got buzzed just running around Yondareth, the world of Dragon Epoch our newest and most interesting method of escape.

I couldn't wait to venture out and see who else shared this gorgeous virtual world. It turned out I didn't have to be so much of a hermit, because we met our first new friend that night—a human healer who went by the name of Persephone, as in the goddess of the underworld. That meeting was a simple matter of her putting up her LFG tag, which denoted her as *looking for a group*, and the two of us being badly in need of healing from our fights.

Heath had created a barbarian mercenary, a huge warrior that towered over my demure, slight elf woman. Fragged was as big and brawny as Heath was in true life, with muscles upon his muscles. As far as I was concerned, he was a hit-point absorbing machine—or as I liked to refer to him, my meat shield.

"Man, this is interesting, but I have some complaints already," Heath said. "Lots of eye candy for the straight dudes to look at. Not so much in the way of hot men for the gays."

"Or the straight girls," I added. "Don't forget us!"

He laughed. "I'm not about to, but I think this game might have. Jeez, look at the double D's on that Valkyrie Mama.

Wow. Wouldn't that hurt running around with all that décor on the front hood?"

I looked over his shoulder at the avatar of an unknown player while our new friend Persephone cackled over the voice chat.

I smirked. "Ten to one says that's a guy playing her. And he used the customization features to make her bigger than Dolly Parton."

"Huh…want to invite her to our group and find out?"

And bingo, I was right. It was a guy—under the age of eighteen. I nearly fell on the floor when Persephone asked him point blank if he was a guy and how old he was. I mean, I seriously had to put my hand over my mic because I was laughing so hard. Even Heath couldn't keep a straight face as he proceeded to befriend the barely-pubescent young man.

We grouped with him again a few times after that first night, too, always making cracks amongst ourselves about the mangos, casabas, melons or whatever fruit we chose to compare them to that night. It's a good thing the bra-makers of Yondareth were industrious enough to invent something for adequate support, even in the days before underwire was a possibility. Fine gnomish engineering at our fingertips!

I'd only allow myself to log on after homework was done, along with the requisite hour or two of studying for the MCAT. Reduced hours at the hospital job due to various scheduling issues made it so that I was fortunate enough to be able to log on every night during the beta test.

Aside from the fact that Persephone really got our humor, we seemed to click immediately. And the more we grouped with her, the better we got to know her.

"Almost out of mana. We need a slight break after the next fight," she announced after a particularly grueling room we'd cleared in a set of underground caves leading up to the Minotaur King's throne room.

We chatted while she regenerated her mana—the blue bar that allowed her to cast her spells.

"So… where are you two at?" She'd already picked up that we were roommates.

"SoCal. You? You must be West Coast since you're in the same time zone."

"British Columbia," replied Persephone.

"Wow, a beer and poutine aficionado, huh?" Heath teased.

"Poutine is disgusting. Beer is everything," she answered.

"You work? Or go to college?"

"Both. I babysit computers by night as a sysop. Simon Fraser University student by day. Sleep is optional."

We gave her our details, along with our real names. She told us her real name was Katya.

I had only dabbled with Massive Multi-Player Online Roleplaying games before this—*cough*, World of Warcraft, *cough*—but now I truly appreciated the appeal of playing with new people. Before, I'd quickly grown tired of "grief" players who got their enjoyment from making life miserable for all other players around them. But the policies and terms of service of this game had made it abundantly clear that this behavior would not be tolerated.

The quests we pursued took us to broader and more dangerous areas that led to still more quests to complete. In fact, the game seemed to be quest after quest after endless quest. And I loved every minute of it, even the tedious ones, because the company was great. Then again, every game had its tedious—but necessary—moments, so at least in this game there was an interesting story behind even the simplest of quests. Like being asked to wander to the next field and pick a bouquet of daffodils for a doddering but kind old elf man in honor of his lost love.

Katya was quickly becoming our go-to girl as we worked together on quests and leveling up. And though we'd come to rely on one another, it became apparent that we needed someone to do more damage so we could kill the monsters faster. It just so happened that I came across that someone— after he nearly got my character killed.

I'd been minding my own business, gathering data on the game for eventual blog material—once the NDA was lifted, of course. That night, I was on my own, testing out how well I could fight solo against the mobs.

Without my two compadres to help me, I began to solo some troublesome gnolls who guarded the entrance to the mound outside their burrow. At my current level, fighting the pair of them was challenging, but I pushed my enchantress skills to their utmost potential.

While I put one of them into a mesmerized trance, I proceeded to beat up on his yipping compadre. The hyena-man got in a few good hits before I polished him off.

Unfortunately, as he fell to the ground and I turned my attention back to the swaying gnoll who awaited my magical wrath, a clueless spearman showed up out of nowhere to help "rescue" me.

The thing about putting mobs into a mesmerized trance is that, once they are awakened, they are mighty pissed off at the person who cast the magic on them. So though this strange little toon with a long white beard began to attack the gnoll on my behalf with his gigantic spear, the hyena-man went after *me* instead!

As a squishy spell caster, I didn't have a lot of hit points. Even just a few hits hurt. A lot.

Dammit, I typed as I managed to fire off a "blurred memory" spell that would wipe away the hatred the gnoll bore for me—but also cause the spearman to get full credit for the kill. *Why are you swiping my gnoll?*

The spearman continued to swing at the hyena creature. He typed back, *I'm helping you. I saw you had two mobs on you. I didn't want you to get killed.*

I fired off my biggest nuke spell and burned down half the gnoll's hit points. *I had it handled. He was mesmerized.*

The spearman—FallenOne, so the bright blue name above his head declared—backed off immediately. *Oh crap, I'm sorry. I thought you had aggro. Couldn't tell you had control of the situation.*

You're such a newb, I replied. *Don't ever hit a mesmerized mob, or you are just kill stealing and mooching experience points from another player.*

FWIW, I'm not sure I've ever seen an enchantress play like that... he replied. *It's a difficult class to solo with.*

As I fired off my last spell and the gnoll's corpse thudded to the ground, FallenOne emoted, bending down on a knee. His private message flashed across my screen. *Apologies, milady. I wasn't trying to steal your mob. How may I make it up to you?*

I tapped my index finger on my lip, thinking. Was he in earnest or just a rookie preteen trying to get into my good graces so I'd cast some nice buff spells on him and send him on his way?

On the other hand, with that spear, his class did a lot of damage per second (DPS). That could be valuable, too... provided he wasn't a newb idiot.

My group could use some DPS, assuming you aren't too much of a newb, I typed.

He emoted a low bow. *I promise not to screw up again.*

I paused. Well, we could "screen" him, I guess. To see if he'd prove himself remotely helpful.

Play with us for an hour. If you're useful, maybe we'll keep you for longer. I bit my lip to fight a wicked smile. Man, I could be such a bitch when I wanted to. But hey, in all probability, he might not even show up.

Tomorrow night, 9 pm PST. Meet us by the city gate and we'll group up.

Without hesitation, he bowed again. *I am your servant, milady.*

My brows arched. He certainly had the period lingo down. Maybe he was more experienced in fantasy gaming than he'd let on with his initial encounter.

I began the process for "camping out" of the game by sitting my character down. It took approximately thirty seconds. Right before disappearing, I replied to him, *We shall see. Tomorrow. 9 pm.*

I finished my day with my regimen of MCAT studying. Two hours today would hopefully make up for working the hospital job tomorrow and then gaming with the group later that night.

Sure enough, when we logged in at our appointed time, FallenOne was online and waiting for us. One minute after appearing at the city gate, he emoted a deep bow.

Surprised—even a little impressed—I rattled off a quick explanation of what had happened to my group members in voice chat. Then, I invited FallenOne to join us.

Unlike Heath, Katya, and me, FallenOne didn't use the voice chat feature. He said it was because his equipment wasn't working.

Maybe he doesn't know how to properly use the voice chat function. He strikes me as a bit of a newb, I opined in a joint private message to Heath and Katya (who had told us we could call her "Kat").

He's probably just shy, Kat replied.

Or maybe he's just a poor student with shitty equipment. Why you girls gotta read into everything? As always, Heath had to "set us straight."

The beauty of MMOs was that necessity made extroverts out of the most withdrawn introverts.

Despite my initial questionable encounter with FallenOne, we ended up finding him very helpful. He had a solid knowledge of the game, which was vital to those of us—read: all three of us—who were still floundering around figuring out how things worked.

The quests are tiered and gated, he explained. *So finish the low level ones first and the higher level quests will open up. They interconnect. Like a web or network.*

We'd only been playing this game for about ten days, so I was amazed. I was also surprised he was still the same level as us. "How do you know so much about this game?" Persephone asked during our first night together as a group.

I get around, was his only answer. *There *was a closed alpha test before this, you know. This might be the closed beta, but the stress beta opens up in just two weeks. You'll all be experts to the open beta people!*

There was a long pause amongst us.

"Ohhhkay. FallenOne, you are officially the mystery man," Heath declared.

Just the way I like it, Fallen replied.

"So I guess this means we don't get to know your a/s/l?" joked Kat.

He answered with a snarky, *a = old enough to know better, s = yes, as often as possible and l = here and there.*

"And Yondareth, of course," I said cheekily. "Where boobs defy gravity and men are hearty, strong and appealing to all. All except those attracted to men, that is," I said, laughing as Heath made a face.

Wait, what? asked Fallen.

Ah, of course he hadn't noticed. Seeing fantasy women dressed so scantily had become so much of a norm, most men accepted it without question. One more clueless male to educate! Girl Geek again gets her hands dirty so that the rest of womankind doesn't have to—unless they want to, that is.

"I just mean that I don't think the game creators realize that women play this game, too."

I'm sure they realize that. Why wouldn't they? But of course they are going to market more to men. After all, statistics are statistics and most players of these types of games are male.

"Pfft. Yeah," I said. "And it will stay that way unless they tone down the skimpy lingerie armor and the ginormous boobies."

I got nothing against ginormous boobies. I love a good pair of boobies.

"Then they should give us some nice bulging packages as a nice counterpoint," Heath said.

"Or glistening abs!" I added.

But as a chick, don't you want your character to be hot in the game?

"Chicks can kick ass, too. Not just be eye candy," Kat pitched in.

I'm sure the game producers would appreciate that kind of feedback from the beta testers. "More eye candy for the female characters."

"Or even better—equal opportunity eye candy! I think I'll submit that in the virtual suggestion box," I snarked. "Too bad it'll be immediately trashed without ever being read."

Hmm. The sarcasm is strong with this one.

"Oh, Fallen, you have no idea," Heath said. "I live with Her Majesty, the reigning monarch of All Things Sarcastic. And believe me, there's a whole lot more where that came from."

"I have outlets for when the sarcasm overfloweth," I said.

I wonder if the game will be able to live up to your incredibly high standards, Eloisa.

"Indeed, the pen is mightier than the sword," Heath replied. "In this case, literally—the virtual pen becomes mightier than the virtual sword of Yondareth."

You're a writer?

I waved Heath off, but he spilled the beans far too soon. "Worse. She's a blogger, my friend."

I flipped Heath the bird across our shared table, and he stuck his tongue out at me.

You blog? About what? Gaming? Photography? Knitting?

Heath bust out laughing, and before he could answer, I interjected. "Heath is not allowed to give further information about my blog on pain of death. *And believe me*, I can make it very painful."

"She blogs about feminism and gaming. See? I'm not afraid of you!" Heath sent me a wink.

I covered my mic and turned to Heath. "He might be one of those male gamer activists. You never know."

Heath muted his own mic and shook his head. "I can recognize those a mile away. They out themselves pretty quickly. FallenOne and I have been chatting in PMs all night. I can tell he's cool."

That actually sounds really cool. Link please. Must read.

Heath looked up at me, brows raised. "See? Besides, it's not like he knows where to find you or anything. These are beta characters. We can dump them anytime and pick new names. *Voila*, any harasser would no longer know where to find us in-game."

I spoke into my headset to Fallen. "No snarky commenting allowed, by the way. And you can't blow my cover. I never reveal my character name or what server I'm on."

But Heath had a point—if Fallen did any of that, it was still early. It also might be a good litmus test for his trustworthiness. If he became a regular in our group, I'd have to know he was worth trusting with sensitive info. What better way than to test it now, when our characters were still disposable?

You don't get harassed or anything, do you?

I shrugged. "Sometimes. Nothing serious though, fortunately." I was lucky. Some women had been seriously harassed for speaking out in the *man's world* of gaming. With threats of violence and cyber-attacks, even. It was awful. I'd been lucky due to my smaller platform.

Heath started typing furiously on his keyboard, and I assumed he was sending Fallen the blog link. Oh well... I put my thoughts up on that blog for all the world to read. Why not the poor shy guy we'd grouped up with for the night?

So how long have you 2 been dating? Fallen suddenly asked.

"Who two?" Heath answered. "Us two?" Heath looked up at me and I started snickering—hard.

"It's not *that* funny." Heath smirked. "Fallen, we aren't dating. We're just mutually adopted siblings and now roommates. I like guys. She doesn't like people at all."

I bit my lip but nodded approvingly at his explanation. "Oooh. Maybe Fallen likes guys, too! Too bad you're taken."

Heath put a hand over his mic and said, "This guy is a docile, middle-aged mailman living in his mom's basement, what do you want to bet?"

I shrugged. I kind of hoped not. FallenOne was intriguing, but his secrecy was worrying. Odds were that Heath was closer to the truth than I wanted to admit.

Kat had been informed earlier in the week about my blog and had told me she'd read some of it and enjoyed it. She'd even asked if I needed a guest poster. Given her playing talent, I'd love to take her on—for no pay, of course.

"There's four of us here in this group. We should recruit a fifth person and start a guild," Kat said suddenly. "We can call ourselves *The Misfits!*"

Heath made a face. "Doesn't sound very period-authentic."

I can't join a guild, sorry, replied FallenOne. *In fact, I have to go. Exhausted beyond words right now. You have all held me hostage with the witty banter tonight. Almost forgot I have to be up reeeaaaally early.*

I frowned at that, checking the clock. Shit, it was already midnight and the time had passed like it was standing still. I had an early morning class the next day. "Ugh, I need to go, too. Chemical Analysis lab in the morning."

You're a chemist?

"Premed," I answered.

"Yeah, she's a brainiac. She wiles away most of her spare time studying, even while I try to lure her away with the promise of gaming. She's a regular party animal, all right."

I bit my lip, accustomed to the description that had been applied to me for years. Yeah, I was an overachiever and proud of it. And I really, *really* had to be, given my aspirations. Some people prided themselves on the flattering descriptions of their appearance. I prided myself on my above-average brain. That alone kept most of the men away. Most men were easily intimidated by an intelligent woman.

"We'll see if it's all for naught once I take the MCAT."

What's that?

"Medical College Admissions Test. The biggie to get into med school. Four more months." I blew out a tight, nervous breath, feeling that familiar wave of nerves hit me. To counter it, I vowed to spend my lunch break the next day studying instead of watching old reruns on TV or logging onto the game.

Well, you all, it was nice meeting you. Maybe I'll see you around again sometime.

"You should group with us again, Fallen," Kat said. "We're lots of fun, and we could use more spearman DPS."

Maybe! I'm kind of a free spirit, but I'll definitely look you up. I've added you all to my friends list.

"Same," Heath replied.

And then he was gone.

"Well, he's a strange one," Heath said as we logged off.

I shrugged. "He's shy. Seems pretty nice, though."

"We'll never see him again," Kat opined. "He'll either move off to another beta test or roll up a new character when he gets bored with this one. One of the problems with MMORPGs is that you meet new people, make friends, hang out, have a lot of laughs and then the person disappears without a trace. I've seen it happen before."

I shrugged. "Well, that would suck, but I guess if that's the way it goes..."

"Okay all, I'm out, too. Good night!" Katya said.

Heath held his arms above his head, stretching. "Night Kat. Time for me to call it, too. I gotta get up in the morning and help Brian get ready to list some of his stuff on eBay."

I raised my brows. "Ah, so he's decluttering to prepare for the move?"

He cleared his throat, looking sheepish and—I think—a little guilty. "Yeah."

I shrugged and gave him a wry smile to help deflect that guilt. "I've got some free time this weekend to go house-hunting. I have a few apartments to check out. I'll report back."

"Let me know if you want me to come along."

"I think you're better off helping Brian. But if I'm having a hard time deciding on a place, you'll definitely be the tie-breaker. Okay?"

He nodded, still not appearing all that happy. I had a feeling he wanted some control over wherever it was I was going to move. But he had to accept that I was a big girl now, and this next step was mine and mine alone to take.

On that note, we hit the sack. And I couldn't completely recall later, but I could swear I had a dream about a gamer nerd who, instead of being a middle-aged balding mailman, was tall, dark-haired and hot. With miles of muscles and a sexy voice.

Ha. As if.

Chapter 3:
The Mystery of FallenOne

"FIFTEEN QUESTIONS: WHAT'S YOUR GAMEOLOGY?"
–posted on the blog of Girl Geek.

So, there's a meme that's been floating around the Gamer sites, and I've been tagged to join in the fun. Why not? Girl Geek is always game for a little fun. (see what I did there?)

Without further ado...

Girl Geek answers Fifteen Questions:

1. What is your gamer tag?

Um. It's GirlGeek. Yeah? Shouldn't surprise anyone!

2. PC or Console?

PC. I don't even own a console. Okay, so my PC is a rusty bucket of bolts, but I'm able to play my favorite games with everything adjusted on the lowest possible graphic display and sound settings. I'm hoping to upgrade soon, but money's tight! At least I can still blog on it, right?

3. Keyboard or Gamepad?

Keyboard. I'm not fancy!

4. Single player or Multi player?

Multi-player, though I do love some single-player games. There's something about the camaraderie of working toward a goal together. I like meeting new people through games, too. I've made some amazing friends through my newest obsession, Dragon Epoch.

5. What was the first game you've ever played?

Final Fantasy—I couldn't even tell you which number it was.

6. Hardest game you've ever played?

Any first-person shooter (FPS) game. 'Cause I suck at them. I never did want to shoot anyone, anyway. I'd rather zap them with my lightning bolts or fireballs instead!

7. What is your favorite game of all time?

Legend of Zelda! Old school is very cool.

8. What game is currently your favorite?

Dragon Epoch is the game that has eaten my life. And I love every second of it, pet peeves and all!

9. Favorite video game genre?

MMORPG, or pretty much any role-playing game.

10. Favorite video game character?

It's a toss-up between Lara Croft from Tomb Raider—because she's badass—and Alistair of Dragon Age Origins, who is dreamy. He may be made of pixels, but ladies, he's perfection.

11. Which video game character do you hate most?

Wirt the Peg Leg Boy from Diablo. Because really, why-oh-why do we keep trusting that little turkey who's been fleecing the heroes of Tristram for years?

12. What gaming systems do you currently have?

My PC, such as it is, is all I need. I'm a PC gamer and proud of it. I'll leave the console gaming to others.

13. How long have you been gaming?

I started gaming my sophomore year in high school when I was out for part of the year due to illness. My BFF introduced me to gaming. He came to live with my family not long after that, and we became co-dependent video game addicts. We tried out everything there is to try, but, like I said, I love RPGs over FPS, while my BFF is not as discerning. Basically, if it has pixels and beeps, he loves it.

14. How long was your longest gaming session?

Uhhh, do I want to come clean about something like this? I have done an overnighter before (as in twenty-four whole hours!).

15. What game have you clocked the most time on?

Hard to say... the old record was Final Fantasy, but given time, I'm certain Dragon Epoch will take the lead. It's quickly becoming an addiction. What can I say? Want to read my true confession? I've never actually typed /played on a game to discover the hours I've spent playing. I'm scared to see exactly how much of my life has been sucked up by gaming! Scared, I tell you. Ignorance is bliss and all that!

So, there's my meme. Hope you've enjoyed it. As always, leave your Qs and As in the comments, but don't razz me about that /played or I'll delete your ass.

***

FallenOne's private message blinked across my screen in a swath of purple text.

*FallenOne tells you, *I read your blog.*

He'd caught me the next day working the game on my own. Heath was still off with Brian, and after I'd spent a few hours on test prep, I needed a break. So I'd gone for a run, and then logged in to attempt to figure out the crafting and trade system in the game.

By far, my favorite parts of the game were the quests and exploration of new territories. However, I expected that my blog readers would have questions about other aspects of the game once it officially released—and the NDA was lifted of course. I'd have to write about how to make armor, how to craft food for your characters to give them maximum strength, stat improvements and hit point regeneration possibilities, how to make bags to carry all your virtual shit around while you kill and loot the monsters, etc.

But I hadn't expected FallenOne to appear twenty minutes after I logged in and send me his blunt message without even a preface.

I stared at the blinking cursor, suddenly and inexplicably nervous.

*FallenOne tells you, *This is Mia, right? This isn't Heath on Mia's character or something weird like that? Maybe you're AFK?*

I blinked, realizing I'd spent so long staring that I hadn't responded, and he now thought I was AFK—*away from keyboard.* I leaned forward, putting my hands to the keyboard.

*You tell FallenOne, *You read the whole thing? Heath just told you about the blog last night!*

Him: *I read fast.*

Me: *You're actually a computer, aren't you?*

Him: *Computers don't have opinions. Anyway, I think it's a really good blog. Better than a lot of those bigger blogs out there. I'm excited to read your posts about Dragon Epoch after the beta test is over.*

Me: *I'm still absorbing the fact that you've read ALL my content. I've been blogging for 2 years. That's a lot of my ranting to read.*

Him: **shrug* I enjoyed it.*

"Masochist," I murmured to myself, not fully aware of why I was grinning so big that my cheeks were starting to hurt.

Our conversation didn't last much longer. He had to go to work, and I had to finish up a few things before my evening shift at the hospital. But he made it a point of finding our group again, despite having warned us that he didn't regularly game with the same people.

In fact, over the next few weeks, FallenOne and I gamed a lot together when the others weren't around. Persephone had a weird-ass work schedule (mostly graveyard shifts operating a big-ass computer system), and Heath was often out with Brian, probably condo shopping. I, on the other hand, was studying for the test, working some small shifts here and there, writing on my blog or, my favorite, gaming. I was *not,* however, sleeping very much. My mind wouldn't shut off enough to let me sleep more than a few hours a night.

I compensated with another addiction: Dr. Pepper. Ahhh...caffeine. Best invention ever.

And FallenOne, my mysterious young man—or middle-aged basement-dwelling mailman, as the case might be—seemed to keep similar online hours to mine. So we started working on side quests that didn't require an entire group to accomplish. All the while, we enjoyed witty banter.

Me: *I'm one hundred percent certain that the designer of this game is a sexually frustrated pre-pubescent teen.*

Him (after a long pause): *What makes you say that?*

Me: *Just look at it. Every chick has the perfect, and I mean *perfect*, rack. Firm, bouncy yet not floppy. Ample. I bet the guy has never even *touched* a female breast.*

Him: *You never know...*

Me: *I know I'm right.*

Him: *So not only are you a brilliant pre-med student, a witty blogger of all things gametastic, but you also are the resident sexpert who can gauge any man's sexual experience based on limited knowledge?*

I blushed, my cheeks burning. If only he knew he couldn't be *further* from the truth. I'd never had sex before. Not even pseudo-sex.

Me: *Do you think I'd reveal all my talents to you at once? Anyway, I have some unpublished articles about Dragon Epoch that will go up once the NDA is lifted. Can't wait to put those out there.*

Him: *What's your verdict so far?*

Me: *It's pretty decent...*

(After a pause)

Me: *Who am I kidding? It's effing awesome. I really am enjoying this game. Just waiting for the other shoe to drop.*

Him: *Other shoe? What do you mean?*

Me: *Just waiting for the game to disappoint me, I guess. It always happens. But it's only been a week, and I have a feeling there's a lot more of Yondareth to explore.*

Him: *Yeah, there's a lot more.*

Me: *How do you know?*

Him: *I have my ways.*

Me: *So how long have you been gaming?*

Him: *Years.*

Me: *Are you a student?*

Him: *You can say that.*

Me: *There you go, being mysterious again.*

Him: *I like being mysterious. About as much as you enjoy being snarky.*

Me: *Well, they shouldn't make it so easy for me. I can go on for days about the insults to feminism that riddle this game. Maybe I'll continue with my theme about the inadequate women's armor and sexually frustrated boys.*

Him: *There you go talking about sex again.*

Me: *...*

Him: *So...are we going to kill stuff or what?*

Me: *We have to work on this quest for General What's-His-Face.*

Him: **yawn**

Me: *Come on, we're only fifth level. Let's go pick some pretty yellow daffodils in honor of his lost love!*

Him: *These quest designers suck.*

Me: *It's romantic. General SylvanWood wants to remember his lost love.*

Him: **sigh**

***

**Elosia has entered the world of Yondareth*

FallenOne and Eloisa make their way out of the city gates with a nod of approval and a thumbs-up from General Sylvanwood. He wishes them well and thanks them for their desire to help him.

"The next meadow over yonder." The general points the way through the city barricade past the forest line. "In that first clearing. They only grow there."

Eloisa turns to FallenOne, the fifth-level spearman who wears only a loincloth and bears a weapon as long as he is tall. He's a strange-looking character with a bald head and a long, snowy beard—a wizened man who, it seems, is not as old as he appears....

Eloisa, on the other hand, is a spiritual enchantress with revealing robes of bright colors, ornate charms and shining, brilliant jewelry crawling up her arms. Her ears might be pointed, but she's far from a tiny figure in a tree who makes cookies and sings. She's more like an eternally young old soul—a protectress. Like the legendary Galadriel.

Into the forest they go, opposing bats and animated skeletons in their way. As they do so, they start to work together. When FallenOne dies in the third battle against a particularly annoying skeleton, Eloisa runs back to the city gate to meet his ghost so they can recover his things together.

"Come on, Fallen, let's make sure this doesn't happen again," says Eloisa.

"I'm sick of dying. I think we should just redo the quest later." FallenOne sighs, his head hanging low with discouragement.

But Eloisa is determined!

"I think we've got the hang of this. Shall we try one more time? If it looks like the mobs are going to kill you, I'll throw myself in the way!"

"Fat lot of good that will do! They'll just come after me once you die."

"No, because you can run fast and dodge them."

As it turned out, neither of them had to sacrifice themselves or die.

They learned to work together. Since Fragged was gone, they didn't have a strong warrior to absorb the damage, and since Persephone wasn't around either, they couldn't benefit from her healing magic.

Rather, they had Fallen's spear to cause damage and Eloisa's magic to slow down the monsters—and enhance FallenOne's fighting ability!

They succeeded...because they figured out a way to do it together.

Eventually, they make it to the clearing in one piece, where they find a field of red poppies with only tiny dots of flowers of other colors—purple violets, bright marigolds and white daisies. Finding the requisite number of yellow daffodils is challenging while fighting off giant bees—with humanoid heads, no less—and one enraged gardener who chases after them, wielding a hoe.

"Look at us," FallenOne says. "We really do make a good team."

"Yes," Eloisa replies. "High Five, spearman!"

And so began their duo adventures, spending time together way too late in the night.

＊＊＊

*You tell FallenOne, Where were you the other night?

　*FallenOne tells you, I had a date. Sorry.

　Me: Oh, interesting...didn't know you had a girlfriend.

It might have been pure assumption that he'd been out with a female, but his previous comments about liking boobs *had* led me to believe that he was heterosexual...so I presumed it was a woman.

Him: *Not really a girlfriend. Just a friend.*

Me (strangely relieved): *Ah. Does she play DE?*

Him: *Nope. No way.*

Me: *Why "no way"? Would you not associate with a gamer chick or something?*

Him: *I associate with you, don't I?*

Me: *Not the same. We aren't friends IRL.*

Him: *It's the same. I consider you a friend.*

Me: *But I bet this girl knows your name. You never tell me your name.*

Him: *You've never asked.*

Me: *You know mine. Quid pro quo, ya know...*

Him: *Quid pro what?*

Me: *Tell me your name. Don't be dense.*

Him: *I'm naturally dense. I'm male.*

Me: *Har har. You've been reading my blog too much. Okay so...spill.*

Him: *My name is FallenOne.*

Me: *You suck. ../.. (that's the virtual middle finger in case you didn't pick it up)*

Him: *You wound me.*

Me: *I don't care.*

Him: *I just like having a mysterious persona.*

Me: *I can tell. Someday soon, I'll pry it out of you.*

Him: *I might even enjoy that.*

Hmm. Okay. Definitely heterosexual.

Wait, was he *flirting* with me? After having gone out on a "date" with a "friend"? I frowned, puzzled. The dating habits of people my age—or presumably my age—still confused me.

Me: *Well anyway, we could become IRL friends and it would be awkward calling you Fallen all the time. And if you ever come out to California, you could hang with me and Fragged. We could show you a good time.*

Him: *What part of California are you in? North? South?*

Me: *South. Not far from LA.*

Him: *Really...*

Me: *You seem surprised. Where are you at?*

Him: *I'm going to opt for being mysterious again.*

Me: *Pffft.*

Him: *Actually, I'm getting super tired. It's 4 am and I'm falling asleep.*

He *really* must have been tired because he just revealed, despite his earlier evasiveness, that he was three hours ahead of me. So that narrowed his state of residence to anything from Maine clear down to Florida, as far east as Massachusetts and as far west as Ohio.

Oh, hell. That wasn't narrowing it down at all...

Me: *Do you have an early class?*

Him: *I have to be out the door at 9. This isn't good.*

Me: *Drink lots of caffeine. Good night!*

Him: *Zzzzzzzzzzz*

As time went by and we got together regularly two or three nights a week, it got harder and harder to pull details out of him. It had become my mission to figure FallenOne out, but even Heath was no help.

And, of course, when Fallen wasn't around and the rest of us were, we'd speculate about him.

"Maybe he's a movie star," Katya said. "I've heard there are famous people who like to play games like these so they can be social while remaining anonymous. I read an article that Henry Cavill was playing World of Warcraft when his agent called him to tell him he got the part of Superman. He almost didn't pick up because he was on a raid!"

I snorted and Heath's only comment was, "If Fallen looks like Henry Cavill, then I call dibs. I don't care if he's straight."

"Seriously," Kat continued. "My favorite author blogs about playing WoW but won't say what character she plays or which server."

Across from me, Heath shrugged. "Maybe he's just some sort of weird recluse."

"He has a girlfriend," I said.

"Shut up!" Kat practically yelled over our voice chat. "Dudes who play this game *don't* have social lives."

Heath blew out a breath. "Screw you. *I* do."

"You don't count," Kat replied. "You date men. You could just get your dates hooked on gaming so you'd have immediate company and no time conflict."

I looked at Heath over my monitor and started laughing. Nothing could be further from the truth regarding Brian. That shithead—a name I only called him in my head lest I hurt Heath's feelings—not only had zero interest in gaming, but he even poked fun at our hobby. Heath had stopped playing altogether whenever Brian was over—a fact which bugged me even more.

"He's probably not a movie star, living on the East Coast," I chimed in. "Maybe a sports figure or—oh hey, maybe he's in DC and works in the government?"

"Maybe he's President Obama. Do you think the Secret Service would let him play?" Kat asked.

Heath snorted. "Obama would never play a half-naked monk. I'd guess the Prez would be more of a Bard sort of character, given the nice speeches he gives."

"Wonder what Michelle Obama would play?" I asked. "An elf badass something-or-other—named FLOTUS, of course."

"Well, FallenOne's probably not your president," said Kat. "So who the heck is he? Someone needs to spark a FallenOne investigation. Heath, are you are man for the job?"

Heath shrugged, staring at his monitor as he took care of some busywork in the game. "I think he's just a weird dude who doesn't like to be social and lies about having a girlfriend."

I frowned. Maybe that was as close to the truth as I was ever going to get. Though for some reason, that really didn't sit well.

The speculation ended there, however, and we agreed that FallenOne would remain a temporary mystery. He was a good player, and we all enjoyed his company. And apparently, despite being a "free spirit," he kept coming back for more.

It wasn't long before our little group was a regular fixture in the game. We all had our real-life jobs. Kat and I—and, I presumed, FallenOne—also had our studies. The others had social lives, too. And those were the hours I filled with study. But when it was gaming time, we met in our virtual space and we played. *Hard.*

We still had many mysteries to discover—in Yondareth, as we leveled up together, and outside in the real world. Maybe one of the mysteries we'd solve would be who FallenOne *really* was.

Chapter 4:
Mia Makes a New Friend

POGO TELLS YOU, *HI. YOU'RE CUTE*
You tell Pogo, How on earth do you know that?

Pogo: *I have eyes. Nice armor.*

Pogo wolf whistles at Eloisa.

Eloisa rolls her eyes.

Loved it when numbskull kids had no ability to tell a fantasy avatar from reality, hitting on hot avatars as if they were real.

***

"Hey… good news. I found a place," I said to Heath as I grabbed the collection of dirty dishes off his desk on the way to the kitchen.

Heath looked up from where he was concentrating on his web design work. It took him a minute to register the news, but he was still chewing on it when I got back from dumping his dishes in the dishwasher. I'd even had time to grab a glass of ice water, which I set down on my desk before sinking into my chair once again.

But when I met his gaze, I realized that he didn't seem as happy or as relieved as I'd expected him to be. He actually appeared skeptical. Leaning back in his chair, he said, "Where is this apartment? South Santa Ana? West Orange?"

Naturally, he'd assumed the worst parts of town. "No." I stuck my tongue out at him. "Actually, downtown in Orange, near the university."

His brows rose. "You win the Lotto?"

"It's a studio above a garage."

"Huh. Well, I'll need to see it before I can approve."

I rolled my eyes and folded my arms over my chest. "I don't need your approval. I am an actual adult, you know." I'd turned twenty-one the previous month, and though I was of drinking age now, I hadn't gone on any benders—nor did I actually feel like the adult I now claimed to be.

And really, Heath was only six months older than me. Since when had he become the boss of me?

His intent gaze was still leveled on mine, unfazed by my protest. "Your mom ordered me to look after you."

I snorted and put my feet up on my desk, grabbing my MCAT study manual. "It's not like I'm some party girl or addict. I'm as close to a shut-in as you can possibly get without, you know, actually being one." As if to emphasize that fact, I gestured to the book I'd just picked up. A book I could practically quote from rote memory, I'd reviewed it so much.

He chewed on his bottom lip, appearing as if he hadn't heard a word I'd just said. "Well... I want to come along, anyway. Just don't put up an argument, okay? I gotta make sure my conscience will be clear."

"You've got nothing to feel guilty about! But okay..."

I sighed. I'd basically already made up my mind, but better to put him at ease. I was determined to move out as soon as possible, absolving myself of any responsibility in their relationship's demise, should it ever come to that. In fact, maybe moving out was my way of making sure *my* conscience was clear.

***

"Nope. No way. You're not living here." Heath stood in the middle of my would-be new studio—such as it was. The place was small but somewhat charming. And it was very clean, at least.

The apartment sat above the garage of a family who lived in a modest home just outside the City of Orange's locally famous historic district. Like the homes around it, this one had been built in the 1920s in the Craftsman bungalow style. Additions had expanded the size, including the single room above the detached garage, where I had every intention of moving.

"Heath." I sighed. "This place is fine."

"It's too small." He glanced over his shoulder to make sure the landlady who had unlocked it for us was out of earshot. "It's above an uninsulated garage, which will make it baking hot in the summer and freezing cold in the winter."

"Freezing cold." I snorted. "This is Southern California."

"Okay, so the temperature is relative. But I give you ten days of a Southern California September in this place, max. It will be like an oven. Also, the water heater is tiny and the pressure is crap."

I sighed...again. Perhaps he had no idea how miniscule my income really was. "I really can't be picky. And besides, I don't need a big place—just enough space for me to study, make a meal, shower and sleep."

He frowned. "But you don't even have furniture or dishes, or any of that stuff."

I walked the perimeter of the room as if to somehow demonstrate that it was big enough for me. "I have a bedroom set already, and Mom says I can go to the ranch and pick up a few pieces of furniture. She's got an old loveseat and a table, if I can borrow a truck to go get them. And some dishes. I don't need a lot. It's not like I'm going to be throwing dinner parties—or *any* type of parties. It's a small place that hopefully will be quiet enough that I can study. If not, I'll have the library just down the street."

He shook his head. "You sure know how to party, doll."

I made a face at him. "Anyway—"

He held up a hand to cut me off. "Okay, okay, I get it. But at least promise me that you won't sign any papers for a little while? I might be able to find you something better."

I failed to see how. I'd scoured all the websites, including Craigslist, called real estate offices, checked with the housing office at the university and had become intimately familiar with pretty much everything in my price range in the area—which wasn't much since my price range was extremely limited. The alternative would be to conjure a roommate out of thin air.

I was confident that if I gave Heath a week, he'd come to the same conclusion I had. He was just feeling guilty about Brian's demands leading me to move out in the middle of the school year. But I wasn't going to let him burden himself like that. So I nodded, but I didn't promise I wouldn't sign.

I'd call the landlady tonight when he wasn't around and stop by tomorrow after my early class to sign the paperwork. He'd be annoyed when he found out but also relieved. And…he'd get over it. Heath had never been one to hold a grudge.

***

Days later, after working the morning shift at the hospital, I resisted the urge to take a nap, though my eyelids were drooping. Thus, I studied at my desk instead of heeding the siren's call to go lie down on the bed. That was a quick invitation to fall asleep with my nose inside my study manual.

Instead, I made a rare cup of afternoon coffee—sure to keep me up too late—and sipped as I ran down the extensive list of item definitions, using my computer to look up additional information on terms I wasn't sure about.

The MCAT contained a series of hypothetical problems that needed to be solved based on background knowledge. So these key terms were essential to know, inside and out, in order to solve the hypothetical challenges.

Every day I made it a point to answer at least five sample questions that I acquired via study materials or the Internet. As I was in the middle of this, a key jiggled in the lock, and I assumed it was Heath returning from Brian's place after having spent the night.

Instead, it was Brian… alone. He scanned the room and then turned to me without any greeting whatsoever. "Heath's not back yet?"

I blinked. Brian was already behaving as if he lived here. Which, for all intents and purposes, I guess he did.

"I thought he was with you," I replied. "And uh, hi, by the way. How are you?" I tagged that on there just to emphasize his rude behavior.

He ignored me completely, carrying the box in his arms straight into Heath's room before returning to the front room empty-handed. "He had to take his Jeep to get it detailed. He's probably still waiting for it. Actually, it's good because it gives us a chance to talk."

He'd never privately addressed me before, nor had he expressed a desire to "talk." And every time he *did* address me, his voice dripped with condescension and misogyny.

I frowned as Brian sank down on the couch, fixing me with his ice-blue eyes. His hair was perfectly styled in the so-called "flippy"—a wanna-be Harry Styles haircut. In fact, he dressed with that careful attention to detail of any man who wanted to look like a skater without ever having been within ten feet of a skateboard.

"You need to lay off the guilt trip with Heath," he started and then tilted his head as if lecturing a child.

I drew back, astonished. "There's no guilt trip. I found a place. He's the one who's objecting."

He shook his head. "Yes, I understand that's what you're *saying...* but the undercurrent is completely different. Heath feels responsible for you, and it *really* is time for you to grow up and move beyond the nest, little chickadee."

My blood boiled, and suddenly it felt as if steam was about to escape my ears. I was sure Brian noticed the flush in my cheeks. *Fuck you, twerp.*

"Well, I'm sorry you feel that way, and you'll be happy to know that I *have* found a place and signed all the papers days ago!" I snapped up my books, notecards and notebook, gathering them in my arms. "And *you* can lay off the bullshit. I realize we don't like each other, but you know what? We both love Heath. And though I'm moving out soon, I will *always* be in his life. So *you* had better accept *that,* little chickadee."

I stood up and stomped to my room, leaving Brian with his eyebrows sky high and his mouth agape. I only *just* resisted slamming the door.

I'd never shown open hostility to him like that before and had taken his needling without response for far too long.

Not anymore.

With a sigh, I realized that, having spilled the beans to Brian, I would now have to come clean with Heath about the studio above the garage. In spite of his aversion to it, he hadn't been able to find me any better prospects—as I'd suspected he wouldn't.

Despite my best efforts, I fell asleep on my bed in less than half an hour, my study session ruined thanks to asshole Brian. When I woke from my nap, the apartment was empty again and it was dark out. I was in no mood to go back to my studies yet, nor did I feel like going running. So to blow off some steam, I logged onto the game.

I wasn't even fully logged in when a message from a complete stranger flashed across my screen.

RageRod tells you, Hey Baby.

Ugh. Really? RageRod?

RageRod tells you, Are you a real girl?

*You tell RageRod, *More real than your toy blow-up doll, kiddo.*

RageRod: *I don't have a blow-up doll.*

Me: *Well then, maybe you should get one and stop pestering every female avatar you see.*

RageRod: *You're totally a dude. They need more real girls playing this game.*

Me: *Because then they'd have to pay attention to you?*

RageRod: *You're not very nice.*

Me: *Perhaps you should tell your elementary school's principal on me. Now... don't talk to me anymore.*

You are now ignoring RageRod

A new message flashed on my screen minutes later as I was in the bank. I almost went ballistic, figuring the douchebag had made a new toon to message me with. Instead, I saw with relief that it was Kat. Just the person to brighten my mood.

*Persephone tells you, *I think FallenOne likes you.*

*You tell Persephone, *What?*

Her: *You heard me.*

I heaved a big sigh.

Me: *Are we back in high school? Besides...why would you think that?*

Her: *Because twice now, he's logged on and grouped up with me for a few minutes before asking where you were. When I said you were in class or busy, he promptly made up some excuse about how he had to go.*

Me: *I'm sure it's a coincidence.*

Her: *Okay. If you say so. But he never logs on asking for me or Fragged.*

Me: *We've already determined that he's kind of weird, though, right? Who knows what goes on in a reclusive gamer dude's head.*

Her: *We should apply the scientific method to my theory sometime, if you are willing.*

Me: */shrugs. Figure out a way to do that and I'm game!*

Her: *Right, I'll start with step one: make an observation. As there is but little background information on our mysterious friend, I have only his in-game behavior to go on. He logs on and asks for you regularly. When you are not available, he quickly logs off. When you are, he stays and plays with you (or with the group as a whole).*

Me: *Sigh. Okay...your inquiry?*

Her: *Does FallenOne have feelings for Mia?*

Me: *And your hypothesis?*

Her: *FallenOne has developed special feelings for Mia... and vice versa.*

Me: *Now you're getting annoying.*

Her: *Prediction based on my hypothesis about FallenOne and Mia. First comes LOOOOOOVE. Then comes marriage. Then comes the baby in the baby carriage.*

Me: *../..*

Her: *Now I must test my hypothesis by asking subtle questions to FallenOne about his love life...and whether or not he believes in cyber romance!*

Me: *Good luck with that. I want no part of it.*

***

Soon after, the Dragon Epoch stress beta test ended. Since there would be no character wipe, we were permitted to continue playing our same characters from the beta. The NDA was lifted, and I was permitted to post to my blog about Dragon Epoch.

In fact, I was in the middle of writing a new blog post when I decided to check my ad revenue. It was nearly time to pay the bills again, and I was furiously working toward the goal of this blog paying for itself—even better if it started bringing in a little spending money.

To that end, I was astonished to note that the balance for my account had undergone a significant increase. This then prompted me to check my stats.

Since posting the new content about Dragon Epoch, the number of hits on my blog had increased by a factor of hundreds. My jaw dropped.

"Holy crap!"

Heath looked up from his work. "What?"

"My blog hits are going crazy. I haven't even blogged about anything controversial or particularly newsworthy lately. It does look like the Dragon Epoch articles are getting the most attention, though."

"Everybody's hungry for info on the new game," he said with a shrug. "You getting lots of Google hits?" He came around the desk to get a look at my screen. "Let me—holy crap that *is* a huge jump in hits! And very sudden, too. See the change from this day to the next? Give me a second to do some backtracking and see where the traffic is coming from."

After a few minutes, he blew out his breath and shook his head. "Wow. Looks like someone over at Draco Multimedia found your blog. You've been featured on their main landing page."

I blinked. "Really?"

"Yup." He smirked. "I wonder if this means they're going to start putting some clothes on the poor naked ladies that have been running around Yondareth up 'til this point?"

I logged into my blog interface to check comments. Dozens of them. Most thoughtful, respectful even. I had to block a few trolls, and I now had a lot of questions to answer.

It took me hours that night to get through them all. The blog had just become a lot more work—with the reward of more money, too. Which was a good thing, really. But yet another demand on my already slim amount of free time.

And I had to admit it was a little creepy knowing that employees at the gaming company responsible for my new favorite obsession were reading my blog—snarky commentary and criticisms included.

Wow.

It was a weird feeling—of validation, gratification, and yeah, of being watched. I sensed that this was my fifteen minutes of fame, so I'd capitalize on it while I could. Besides, I needed the money for my move, so I'd welcome the attention with open arms.

I threw a glance at Heath, who had gone back to his work. I'd told him about signing the papers to move into the new place, since I'd already spilled the beans to Brian. Heath had been a little miffed at first, but he'd recovered, fortunately. And I'd refrained from repeating Brian's shitty little remarks.

However, since I wouldn't have access to a moving truck until the next weekend, my plan was to slowly move a box or two over the next little while. The landlady, Lupe, was nice enough to allow me to do it, even though my contracted move-in date wasn't for a few weeks due to the apartment getting a repaint and carpet cleaning.

I couldn't deny, though, the little thrill I got about having my very own place. Tiny studio or not. It would be mine. All mine.

***

A few days later, I schlepped yet another box, this one full of books, to my new apartment. I was just coming down the stairs when I ran into—almost literally—a young woman about my age. When she got over her initial shock of seeing me, she smiled widely and stuck out her hand.

"Hi! I'm Alex. You must be the new tenant." She looked me straight in the eyes without the snotty once-over that some women my age seemed to give when seeing someone new. Their eyes skimmed a new person from head to toe, cataloging every scrap of attire as if running it through a super-fast computer—like the one inside Iron Man's suit. But Alex's eyes did none of that.

I took her hand and shook it. "Hi, Alex. I'm Mia." Her impossibly wide smile extended even further and she leaned forward enthusiastically. I hadn't met someone this overtly friendly in a long time.

"I'm your new landlady's daughter." Alex was a pretty girl with long, dark hair, an olive complexion and impossibly large, almost anime-like doe eyes. And her make-up was applied to perfection. "And you're a Browncoat!" Her voice glided up an octave on the last word as she pointed to my *Firefly* t-shirt.

I looked down, suddenly feeling a little self-conscious. "Yeah, that's me... Mal and Inara forever!" I've always loved a strong female who stood up to the object of her ongoing attraction, in spite of his outspoken protest of her profession.

"High-five!" She held her hand up and I gently slapped it. "Girl's got taste. Great 'ship! I'm all about the Kaylee/Simon 'ship myself!"

I grinned. I liked her already. Any girl immediately zooming in on my geeklove had my immediate respect.

"Next question," she said, shifting her stance. "Who's your favorite Doctor?"

I laughed. "That's easy. The ninth!"

She pumped a fist. "Woo-hoo. Love it! You're coming to my next drinking party! I live in Fullerton. Since you're down here in Orange, I assume you're attending Chapman?"

I nodded. "Yep. I'm a junior. You?"

"Sophomore at Cal State Disneyland." Her crooked smile accompanied California State University Fullerton's popular nickname. "It's great to meet you, Mia. I gotta run before my mom comes out here and asks me to do something else for her." She rolled her eyes. "But I'll be back for dinner next week. You'll be moved in by then, yeah?"

"Once the apartment's ready, yes!"

"Okay well, I'll definitely see you around! Take care."

I smiled and watched her hurry toward the curb where her car was parked. Well, that was encouraging. Not even moved in yet and I'd already made a potential new friend.

Making my way to my car, I couldn't help but feel grateful. The landlady seemed nice and her daughter equally so. Maybe this was a sign of good things to come! Maybe it was a good thing I was being forced out from under the protection of my surrogate big brother to stretch my wings. Hopefully soon, I'd become a productive member of society. Now I just needed to ace the MCAT.

Piece of cake, right?

***

*FallenOne tells you, *Hey, you!*

I looked up at my notifications, eyes widening. It was late morning and Tuesday was my lightest day—only one class and no shifts at work. I'd logged on to do some virtual banking in the game and to check to see if there was any armor in the auction house that I could buy for my character.

With a small thrill I noted, if only to myself, that FallenOne had logged in right after me.

*You tell FallenOne, *Well hello, stranger! You haven't been around much lately.*

Him: *TONS of work to do. Sorry.*

Me: *Well, you missed the grand opening of the game. The beta test is a done deal! And the wave of newbs has flowed onto the servers...*

Him: *So I noticed. But people seem to be liking it a lot.*

Me: *What's not to like? Fun part is that the NDA has been lifted, so now I can post about it!*

Him: *I've seen that! I'm still reading the blog.*

Me: *You and a lot of other people. It's getting me so swamped. But that's a good thing, even though it's cutting into game time. Hardly gotten a chance to run around since the opening.*

Him: *I've got a little bit of time this weekend…*

Me: *Ugh. I don't. Sorry. Going up to my Mom's for the weekend. I'm moving out soon!*

Him: *Congrats! You moving in with roommates or a special someone?*

I raised my brows. Was that his way of trying to find out if I had a boyfriend? I bit my lip, thinking back to Katya's suspicions.

Me: *Nope. There is no "special someone" in my life. I'm moving because Heath's boyfriend wants to move in with him.*

Him: *Ah, okay. I hope you have lots of help moving. Maybe I'll see you around next week?*

Me: *Sure. You want to just text me when you're free, and I can see if I can hop on? You know it would be so cool if you could send a message to someone in the game, and if they're not online, it would just appear as a text on their phone.*

Him: *That's a pretty good idea.*

Me: *Yeah, but maybe they can't do that. I'm sure they would have implemented it if they could. I can't possibly have been the first person to come up with that.*

Him: *Why not put it into the beta-tester suggestion box?*

Smiling, I didn't mention having tried that a couple of times already and receiving nothing but crickets in response.

I sent Fallen my VOIP number, which forwarded texts to my new prepaid cell phone—just in case of the unlikely event that he was a stalker or something. I'd known him for months and he seemed normal, but... you could never be too safe where the Internet was concerned.

An hour later, a text from him showed up on my phone. And thus, we started texting, off and on, semi-regularly. Maybe a significant friendship *could* grow from randomly meeting on the Internet... you never could tell.

I had to admit I did Google the number to see if I could find out anything more about him. It was a dead end, though, *of course.* The area code was from some place in the panhandle of Texas.

And he didn't strike me as a cowboy. Or an armadillo. Stymied again.

Chapter 5:
Bad News

MY MOM LIVED IN A LITTLE TOWN IN THE mountains just above Temecula, about a two-hour drive from where I attended college in the City of Orange. The following weekend, Heath drove me there in a borrowed truck to fetch a few pieces of old furniture and bring back some supplies for my new apartment. In the end, I think he was relieved that things had been resolved so easily.

Of course, Brian had been ecstatic that I was on my way out. Yeah, sensitive to Heath's torn feelings on the matter, he was not. *Asshole.*

Nevertheless, for Heath's sake, I wished them well together, though I had my doubts that they were compatible. Sure, they were attracted to each other, but they fought like Mario and Bowser. I said nothing because Heath seemed hopeful about the move and the relationship. During our drive, he chatted about their plans to buy a condo up in the Orange Hills. As bad as it was, all I could think of was who would get to keep it when they broke up.

"Mom!" I called as I entered through the front door. She was in the kitchen and pushed through the double doors hurriedly to greet us.

"There they are. My twins!"

She'd given us that nickname in high school. I'd hated it at first but now thought it was funny. Heath and I could not look less alike. Where he was tall, brawny, blond, and fair, I had dark hair, brown eyes, and a tall but lithe figure. And, thanks to my Greek roots, my skin was slightly more amenable to tanning than his ruddy Norse heritage had afforded him.

As I hadn't seen my mother in almost two months, I held her tight in a bear hug. She seemed… thinner. And when I pulled back and looked in her eyes, she looked tired. There were bags under her eyes and she was a little pale.

I also hadn't missed the lack of cars parked in the side driveway. "Where are the guests?"

"Oh, I closed bookings for a bit to give myself a little break." Her dark eyes darted away from mine. "Spring cleaning and all that…"

I frowned but didn't press it. Why close down the B&B during high season? And here, spring was *definitely* the height of the season. The high desert early spring was *not* to be missed. Beautiful flowers of every imaginable color carpeted the desert for a short period of time—sometimes only two or three weeks before the scorching sun desiccated the plants. It usually brought the crowds in droves this time of year.

Mom prepared our favorite meals, and Heath took full advantage of the flora being in full bloom, indulging in his photography passion. One day he even took off on an hour-long drive out to Anza-Borrego State Park. His photos had been getting better and better, and he'd been taking classes to improve his craft.

As usual, he deftly avoided seeing his own parents, despite the fact that they only lived six miles down the road from Mom.

I spent my time helping Mom air out the rooms and give them all a deep cleaning. We stripped bedding and washed it, dusted along ceilings and light fixtures, scrubbed baseboards, and even washed the windows.

We were finishing up one of the cottages—Roy Rogers, our premium room. She was polishing the small rustic table set up as a writing desk, while I was on the ground wiping down the baseboards.

"You're old enough now that I'm going to feel guilty not paying you an honest wage for all this free labor," she joked.

I shrugged and smiled. "It feels good. Gets my mind off things."

"Your exam?"

I shrugged. "Yeah… that… and other things."

It had been bugging me since yesterday, actually. The emptiness of the B&B, the hollowness in Mom's cheeks. Something was going on. Something she seemed to be hiding from me.

I bit the inside of my cheek. Did people *do* that? Hide important things—possibly even unpleasant things—from their family members?

I'd have to find a way to pry the truth out of her. But should I be subtle and poke around the subject or just point-blank ask?

"Anything you want to talk about?" She wiped the last bit of polish from the wood and sat back to watch me. I ran a clean cloth over the baseboards one more time.

I took a deep breath and let it go. *Point-blank it was…*

"Yeah, actually there is."

Mom put aside her rag, looking at me expectantly.

I raised my brows. "I want to know why you look so tired. And I want to know how you hurt yourself."

She blinked. "How I hurt myself?"

I pointed to the bandage on her upper arm that had slipped, now visible at the bottom of her short-sleeved t-shirt. Mom's mouth thinned to a faint line.

Then she swallowed. "I don't want you to get worried about something that might end up being nothing."

I stiffened, and suddenly there was a cold lump of fear in my throat.

"*What?*" I ground my teeth when she didn't respond right away. "Don't try to brave this alone. Tell me, Mom."

She sighed. "But you've got so much on your plate, and it's…potentially nothing at all."

I folded my arms stiffly across my chest. "Which means that it's potentially *something*." I grimaced at her. "Spill it, Mother."

"I had a couple moles on my arm—a group of little birthmarks, actually. They started to look funny, so the doctor wanted to remove them and have them biopsied."

"*What?*" I shot to my feet. "What kind of biopsy? Punch? Excisional? Are you seeing an oncologist?"

Mom held out a hand. "Calm down, Mia. I'm fine. It could be nothing."

"Then why are you looking so tired? Why cancel the guest bookings?"

Her jaw tightened and then she shrugged. "Just a little stress. Nothing else. It's been a rough couple weeks of worrying. But the doc is very optimistic that it's nothing."

I frowned, biting my lip. "But what if it *isn't* nothing? I've been working with an oncologist, you know, doing research this year. I could talk to him more about this, get more information."

She frowned, the creases on her otherwise smooth forehead deepening. "You're freaking yourself out. I learned this week never to Google symptoms, and I don't want you doing the medical student equivalent, okay? I'll get the results later this week—"

"You're calling me the minute you find out." It wasn't a question.

She smiled. "Of course."

"Mom, you need a plan...in case the test comes back positive."

She shrugged. "Do people die of skin cancer?"

I swallowed a giant boulder in my throat. *Yes,* I wanted to say. *All the time.* It's insidious and wretched. Skin is the body's largest organ—by far—and it plays a very important role. Because of that, skin cancer could spread quickly. And once cancer metastasized...

If it was melanoma, God help us. It *couldn't* be melanoma. With everything in me, I willed it to be one of the less aggressive versions of skin cancer. But the description of the dark birth marks, the change in appearance, the location on her arm... All these pointed to the deadliest form of skin cancer out there.

"Was there ulceration? Bleeding? Tell me everything."

She told me, and as she did so, I blinked and swallowed, ignoring the tears rising up and poking the backs of my eyes. I fought to ignore the feeling of having just been kicked in the stomach.

What if…what if I lost her? Aside from Heath, my mom was my only family.

I held it together—barely—for another hour as I tried to act natural while we finished what we were doing. But then I told her I was going to take a long walk.

I took my favorite hike in the hills that surrounded the ranch, to the lookout spot where I always loved to watch the sun set. It was peaceful up there… quiet. I could hear the wind and my own thoughts and not much else.

I did a lot of thinking and still the possibilities swirled in my mind, making me more and more afraid about the future. I was so worked up that by the time I got back, I went straight to the barn to hang out with the horses until Heath got back from his photography excursion.

When he finally pulled up, I flagged him down in the driveway and broke the news to him in the barn. He was much calmer than I was about it, though he did have lots of questions. And he succeeded in calming *me* down, too.

We'd wait for the results. We wouldn't jump to conclusions. We wouldn't borrow trouble.

***

It took us half a day to move my measly belongings into the new place. Another half a day for me to unpack and get settled in.

The day after moving me out, Heath took off on a camping trip in the High Sierras with Brian. Their last little getaway before moving in together—as if they wouldn't be together all the time now. Heath offered to cancel it, but it had been a chore for him to convince metrosexual Brian to indulge in some of Heath's greatest loves—camping, hiking and fishing. I didn't have the heart to foil that plan, so they left with my blessing.

Which meant that, when the news came in... I'd be on my own. And that thought seemed to compound the stress I was already feeling.

"There's going to be someone out to repair the phone line next week," my landlady informed me as I finished emptying the last of the boxes. "There's been a lot of static on the line."

"Wait, there's a landline?" Suddenly, I was overjoyed at the thought of not having to burn through my pre-paid cell phone minutes.

"Yes. It's included in the rent."

This place was becoming more and more affordable all the time. And to top off the good news, the bargain Internet package I'd ordered was up and ready to go the next day.

But as the week drew to a close, I grew more and more tense, texting Mom frequently to find out if she'd had any updates on her tests. She hadn't.

While I waited, instead of studying for the MCAT—like I should have been doing—I spent all of my free time grinding on the game. FallenOne happened to be around, too, and he checked in with me daily.

After the third day, he brought it up.

*FallenOne tells you, *Don't you have that test coming up soon?*

My stomach dropped. I was so preoccupied with worrying about my mom, I'd put the test out of my mind. I told myself that I knew a lot of the basics, right? That it was my simple deductive skills I'd need in order to apply them to the hypothetical situations for the test. Logic and reasoning. I had those. I used those skills almost every single day.

In fact, I was using those skills at this very moment to justify not studying.

*You tell FallenOne, *Yeah...*

Him: *Do I need to tell you to log off the game to study?*

Me: *You can tell me whatever you want. Doesn't mean I'm going to listen to you.*

And I didn't. I kept grinding away. That week, I needed the distraction of the game to get me through.

Because on Thursday, Mom called. And no, the news wasn't good.

I could hardly believe my ears, those words "tested positive for melanoma" echoing in the back of my head, all through my brain. I'd done as she'd asked and avoided Googling all the possibilities. But I *had* had a discussion with Dr. Martin, the physician whom I was assisting with a research project. We discussed the process of diagnosis, the possibilities of what she might have and the preferred protocols for treatment, so I was armed with at least a little knowledge.

"They don't want to do radiation, but...they do want me to start chemotherapy. They are concerned because the margins weren't clear on the biopsy."

Oh God. I bit my lip and rocked back and forth in my chair as I listened to her calm voice drone on. She sounded *remarkably* calm, in fact, for someone who had just received this news. No clear margins meant the doctors weren't sure they'd gotten it all when they'd removed the moles.

"Mia? Still there?" she asked as I struggled to get hold of myself.

"Yeah," I said—a little breathlessly.

"Dr. Shuman is confident that with this course of action, I'll have a great outcome."

I swore I could hear every beat of my heart in my eardrums and every breath that I took in.

"Mia…it will be okay."

I closed my eyes and bit my tongue so I wouldn't speak the words that rested there. She had no idea whether it would be okay or not.

I begged off soon after, using the truthful excuse that I was almost out of minutes. But I really did it because my mom didn't need to hear me break down over *her* news.

Oh shit. Oh shit. Shit. Shit. I could lose her. That was a very real possibility. But as I went through my normal household tasks—washing the dishes, tidying up—I didn't cry. Instead, I went numb inside.

I ended up practically pulling an all-nighter on DE. I went on a leveling binge and didn't care how far ahead I got from my friends. Not long after I hit level 35, a familiar notification flashed onto the screen.

*Your friend, FallenOne, is online.

*FallenOne tells you, *Hey, you're on late...and...wow. Congrats on all the new levels. Planning on letting us catch up anytime soon?*

*You tell FallenOne, *Not in the mood. You might need to bark up someone else's tree.*

Him: ...

Me: *Really having a bad night over here.*

Him: *What's up? Can I help?*

Me: *Not unless you have a miracle cure for cancer in your back pocket.*

Him: *Cancer? Okay, now I'm worried. What's going on?*

Me: *Bad news. Someone I care about has cancer.*

Him: *Do you want to talk about it? I can call...*

Me: *That's kind of you, but I have no minutes left this month.*

Him: *No landline?*

Me: *Oh actually, I do have one at this new place.*

My fingers hovered over the keyboard, hesitating. Did I really want to open up this can of worms? It seemed so much simpler and almost fun to have a mystery friend—one I knew very little about, but who could be there for me. It was a little romantic, actually, the thought that we could be friends like this without romantic feelings getting in the way.

I kind of liked that idea and found myself a little reluctant to give it up—even if it was just a phone call.

But, on the other hand, Heath was up in the mountains above Yosemite, out of cell phone range, and there was no one else I cared to vent to. Suddenly, I realized I wanted to vent. I *needed* to.

And...who was I shitting...I was still morbidly curious about FallenOne. Maybe I'd even get a real-life first name out of him.

After finding my new phone number on Lupe's information sheet, I sent it in a message to Fallen.

A few minutes later, the phone rang, and my hand shook as I answered it.

"Hello?"

"Hi," a deep, distinctly male voice responded. A weird little shiver ran down my spine when I first heard it, and I had no idea where it came from. Was it nerves? *Attraction?* I didn't know.

The line immediately started to crackle, and I remembered Lupe's warning that it needed to be repaired.

"Sorry about the static… apparently, this is a bad line."

"Yeah, it sounds like shit," he said. "Are you okay?"

"Um, yeah. Kinda."

"Do you want to talk about it?" His voice sounded a little garbled, but I could still understand him.

"I don't know. Heath's not here and I don't have anyone else to talk to, but I'm not sure I have anything to say besides this isn't fair and life sucks."

"Life definitely isn't fair."

If I lost Mom, I'd lose all the family I had except for Heath. That thought brought sudden tears to my eyes, and for the first time since receiving the news, they spilled onto my cheeks with such force that I couldn't blink them back. It was like opening a floodgate.

Fallen let me sob without saying anything. I could hear him take a breath every now and then, but mostly I was just drowning in my own misery.

"I'm sorry," I finally wailed into the static after almost ten minutes of sobbing. "It's my mom…"

"Oh shit. I'm sorry."

"It fucking sucks."

"Yeah, it does. Will she be okay?"

I gulped. "I don't know…" The static roared up again, and I could barely hear what he said next.

"I can't hear you," I said.

The static persisted, and I pulled the receiver from my ear and waited. And waited.

And waited.

Finally, I glanced at my screen and saw he'd typed a message to me in-game:

*FallenOne tells you, *Your phone is a piece of shit. I had to hang up.*

*You tell FallenOne, *I know…sorry! But thanks for calling…I guess I needed to get that out.*

Him: *I suspect you have more steam to blow off. Let's go kill stuff. It will make you feel better.*

Me: *Thank you for calling. But I don't want to keep you. It's gotta be *really late there.*

Him: *I am more than happy to be there for a friend—even a friend with a shitty phone line.*

I laughed through the residual snot and tears. Then we headed straight for a high-density area in the game to grind on mobs without doing any quests. We just camped our spot and waited for them to spawn so we could beat them down. We got by without a tank or a healer. Just perfect teamwork. And we did this for *hours.* In the downtime, we chatted.

We'd just finished a particularly close call, and I had to wait to get the mana back for my spells. Eloisa ate and drank virtual sustenance to help with the process.

Him: *I hope you've had a chance to spend time with your mom. I mean, I know you have a really full schedule but...that's important. Just for her to understand how you feel. Don't let anything go unsaid.*

Me: *We are close, but thanks for the reminder. I won't let anything go unsaid...*

My fingers hesitated on the keys before continuing to type.

Me: *Sounds like you're speaking from experience...did someone you love get sick?*

Him: *Yes. Someone I loved very much.*

Loved. Past tense...

So FallenOne had lost that person in his life. My chest ached with sympathy and the knowledge that there, but for the grace of the universe, did I go.

Me: *I'm sorry. I hope you're doing okay.*

Him: *I hope for nothing but that your Mom will be fine. But...just remember not to hold back, okay?*

Me: *Did you hold back?*

Him: *Yes. And I regret it. Every day of my life.*

A lump formed in my throat. He didn't give details about his own loss, just empathized and listened while I typed out paragraph after paragraph of my own fears and worries.

Having someone to be with at this time helped so much. If I couldn't have Heath give me one of his famous bear hugs, at least I could have FallenOne's virtual presence.

It was a surprising place from which to receive comfort.

He stayed online with me until dawn. At some point, after the sun had risen, I woke up with my face smooshed into my desk. I jiggled the mouse to wake up the screen and saw that he had logged off, but only after several messages went unanswered, the last of which was...

*FallenOne tells you, *I suspect you're asleep. Or at least hope that's the case. I'm about to collapse myself, but please send me a text when you wake up so I know you're okay.*

I crawled over to my bed and fell unconscious within minutes, but before I felt sleep take me, I was warmed at the thought of Fallen having stayed up all night with me to keep me company.

And yet, after all that, I still had no idea what his name was.

Chapter 6:
Fallout

"INVISIBLE WOMEN" –POSTED ON THE BLOG OF GIRL GEEK.

An Open Letter to Draco Multimedia Entertainment...and the leadership thereof.

Gentlemen,

And I address this unironically because I can only assume there are no women within five hundred feet of your offices. Or if there are, then they are as invisible as your female players.

"Female players?" you ask, eyebrows climbing your masculine foreheads in astonishment.

Yes. We exist. But as far as you are concerned, we are invisible. Or we are nominal, collateral damage in your quest to market your product to the boys. Because if you do dare acknowledge us in your marketing materials, somehow the boys will feel alienated from all that "icky girl stuff."

But let me clue you in on a little something...our dollars spend just as well as those who carry their genitalia on the outside.

So, why all the scantily clad bikini babes? Why the Amazon sexpots with oodles of bare skin exposed to the elements? There is no such equivalent among your male characters. Or if there is, I have yet to find it. Is there a Chippendales in Yondareth? Equal opportunity skin exposure, please!

*The male-centered storylines and male-oriented quests are ubiquitous. Rescue the fair maiden? Win the longest, biggest sword? *wink wink* Win a kiss from the young maiden named victorious in the village beauty contest? *gag**

I often receive private messages in-game from guild members and others, asking if I'm really a girl "IRL." And of course, the obligatory, "got a boyfriend?" once I answer accordingly. Because, naturally, I'm on the game to find a boyfriend. That would be the only reason I'd be interested in all things geeky, right?

Heaven forbid that a girl can be a girl AND a geek. Because girls who are geeks are just pretending in order to get attention.

I realize this is a symptom of a much larger problem. Female gamers are not treated as equals, are not given characters and storylines that parallel the male-oriented ones. Female gamers are not recognized or even really valued in the community as a whole.

But Dragon Epoch has an opportunity to do its part in reversing this belief. And I call on the lofty male voices at HQ to do so.

Here's my official challenge to the creators of my current favorite game: Do better. Think outside the box. Remember that almost half your player base is, indeed, female. And we don't want to be invisible anymore.

With best regards,
Girl Geek

***

This blog post had been a long time coming…and as a result of the insults against womankind that I'd suffered in-game, DE and elsewhere. Days later, I was still dealing from the fallout of it.

I'd been called out by the male-run blogs and other avid supporters of Dragon Epoch, claiming that "it was all in my head" with a hefty helping of mansplaining on the side. I had to turn off comments on my blog post, block multiple harassers on my social media sites and stop looking at my inbox because of the angry comments—and even some threats.

It was not a good week for all of this to happen. Not after Mom's bad news and the MCAT looming ever closer.

I tried—hard—during the time I would have been working on the blog or on social media to get into the right frame of mind for the test. I knew the material backward and forward, but getting myself to focus long enough to work through the hypothetical problems was another thing entirely.

It didn't help that my hours at the hospital increased significantly due to the oncoming summer season. Though I welcomed the diversion from my own depression over Mom's news and the associated increase in my paycheck, I hardly had any time to study.

And less time to sleep.

And no time to game.

Fortunately, FallenOne kept in touch with me every day via text message. And I looked forward to every single one.

Hey, he'd chime in at some ungodly hour. *You doing okay?*

Yeah. Busy as hell, I replied.

Test coming up soon, right? You all ready to ace it? I could almost hear the smile in his voice—what little I remembered of that deep, smooth, and yeah, a little sexy, voice coming through the crackling phone line.

I'll settle for marginally succeed. The MCAT is specifically designed to eliminate 75% of all medical student candidates who sit for it.

Well, that's a cheery thought. But hey, Heath did say you were a brainiac.

Heath knows nothing. :p

You've been studying for this thing, for what? Two? Three months?

Every day for four and a half months, yes.

You got this. I'm cheering for you.

Are you waving little pompoms and shouting out fun rhymes?

Something like that. Good luck, Mia.

When Heath returned from his trip, he showed up at my door. The camping hadn't gone as planned. Brian had complained during most of it, so Heath decided to spend some time away from him by hanging out in my "dive" (as he called it). It was good to have him with me in my time of need.

But between the extra hours at the hospital, the last-minute, frantic studying and school itself, I was spread really thin. And exhausted.

A week later, the day of the test arrived.

I dragged myself out of bed early, guzzled caffeine and carted my five sharpened number-two pencils and scientific calculator with me.

Hours later, I walked out of that room feeling like I'd been hit by a bus. Crushed. Flat. Broken.

I'd been warned.

The MCAT has often been referred to as a colossal mindfuck. Many a student walked out feeling like they'd utterly failed. Basically, how I felt.

But I was reassured by numerous online MCAT forum posts discussing how they dealt with the aftermath—and the thirty-one day wait for the results.

It would be sheer hell to wait for those results. But I was in good company—feeling like I'd failed while hopeful that I'd known my shit. It had been difficult to concentrate on the problems and my mind had continued to drift.

But I'd finished early…

That was a good sign, right?

I'd find out in thirty-one days.

Chapter 7:
Test Results

T HE WAIT WAS KILLING ME. *KILLING. ME.*

Gaming online wasn't helping much because Fallen was gone for the next three weeks on some mystery trip, Kat was on sporadically, and Heath was in the final stages of buying his new condo.

Yeah, I worked a lot of hours, but I no longer had school, as we were on summer break. So I found myself needing something more.

That led me to actually hanging out with people my own age…in the same room…face to face.

And, astonishingly, enjoying it!

"Waters rise!" Alex practically shouted as she turned over a new card.

"Ah, c'mon, Alejandra. Again? You're practically a flood jinx." Jenna, Alex's roommate, sighed.

I regarded Jenna, who sat across from me. She was gorgeous with pale blond hair—complete with a lone dark teal streak— and serene blue eyes. She twirled one of those platinum strands around a long, thin finger. I had just met her the week before, while still under post-test shell shock, so we didn't immediately click. She was more reserved than the boisterous Alejandra, but tonight I found myself slowly warming to her.

My eyes dropped from her to the cards laid out in a tile pattern on the table between us. Alex puzzled over how to play the cards she'd pulled while Jenna leaned forward, giving her ideas. As Forbidden Island was a cooperative game, we all had to work with each other rather than against.

Jenna seemed almost oblivious to the two males at the table, who were practically drooling over her. According to Alex's gossip, Jenna was dating both of them at the same time. If that was true, she was managing them both like a pro right now and not even sweating it a little.

Or maybe it *was* just an unfounded rumor.

"So Mia, are you seeing anyone?" Alex asked.

I stopped myself from raising my eyebrows in surprise as I drew my three adventure cards and laid them out on the table in front of me: *goblet, statue, statue.*

I cast a wary glance at the guys, whom I barely knew, and said, "No one in particular."

No reason to go into the fact that I *never* dated or the reasons behind it. This wasn't the place to bring up the nightmarish ex-boyfriend and the horrible incident in high school.

"I'm between boyfriends myself," Alex said with a smirk at Jenna. They exchanged a knowing look, sharing an inside joke. Alex was actually sitting between Jenna's two boyfriends. The whole thing appeared lost on the guys, whose names I couldn't remember. "Okay, Mia, draw your flood cards."

"Some people are really good at moving from one relationship to another with ease," Alex said. "I'm not one of those. I need recuperation time in between." She shot a pointed glance at Jenna, who just as pointedly ignored her. "I guess not all of us are in search of Mr. Right."

"Mr. Right?" Jenna said. "You're actually looking for a knight in shining armor. You were born about four hundred years too late for that, chica."

Alex rolled her eyes and told Jenna to take her turn.

The girls were a lot of fun, and I was actually learning from them. Learning that I could always use more friends. Of course, I had my online virtual friends and Heath. But they couldn't always be there for me, and I couldn't expect them to be.

Everybody had their own lives—and I had mine, such as it was.

But sometimes, I was finding, things could get lonely.

So in forcing myself to open up more with new friends, I was learning the value in opening myself up to new relationships. New experiences.

It didn't mean I was going to go out searching for a boyfriend any time in the near future, no matter what Alex said. No need to go crazy!

***

A few weeks later, Heath showed up at my house to mooch the Internet from me, ironically enough. He and Brian had just moved into their new place—a nice two-bedroom condo in the hills—and his wasn't installed yet. So tonight would sort of be like old times, us gaming together in the same room.

"You all ready to go? I think we agreed to working on Kat's complete heal spell quest." Heath checked his watch. "We're meeting online in an hour."

"Yeah," I said. "Logging on to check if the MCAT scores are up today. Officially, they don't go up 'til tomorrow, but word on the street says that they are sometimes available after end of business the night before."

"Well, log in, then! Let's check it out. You were saying you felt like you did okay..."

"I have no idea how I *really* did." I'd just gone with reassuring myself over and over again whenever my mind wanted to scream out that I'd failed spectacularly.

Suddenly, there was a rock in my stomach. What if I'd bombed it? There was no doubt I'd been distracted while I took the test. On the other hand, I had a good command of the vocabulary and background knowledge. Could I have really screwed up that badly on the application of it all? Ah, the MCAT mindfuck at work...

I nudged the keyboard away from me. "Wait...wait. I'm not sure. I kind of like not knowing."

Heath pushed the keyboard closer to me. "Better to know. You ace every test you take, anyway. The best friend a guy could hope to cheat off in high school."

I nodded and took a deep breath, navigating to the Association of American Medical Colleges website and using my account info to log in. It seemed to take forever to pull up my scores. And when they did appear, my stomach dropped. Then I hit refresh, unable to believe my eyes.

"Eighteen," I barely squeaked out. Even *I* could hear the disbelief in my shivering voice.

"Is that good?" Heath asked, every muscle tensing as if poised to jump up and pull me into his arms in a congratulatory bear hug.

"It's terrible," I rasped. "It's beyond terrible. It's abysmal. It's..." My words stuck in my throat and nausea threatened.

"It can't possibly be that bad," Heath scoffed. "It's eighteen out of...what?"

"Forty-five," I croaked. "I performed in the bottom twentieth percentile."

He cleared his throat, a worried look on his face. "Well, surely it's salvageable with your grades, right? I mean you have straight A's in every class. You've never even had an A minus."

I shook my head, my eyes flooding with tears. "Not even my grades can save this. It's give-up-my-med-school-dream bad." I gasped for air. I hadn't been confident that I'd performed perfectly...but I had no idea how low I'd sunk.

How was I ever going to tell Mom? That rock only grew heavier as I thought back to that time, a month before, that I'd taken the test. How could I have been so off base? To have performed this poorly, and yet I had absolutely no clue that I'd bombed it to this magnitude. Talk about a double-whammy.

Heath straightened, watching me closely as I fiercely blinked back my tears. He'd seldom seen me cry, and I'm certain that it disturbed him greatly to see how close this was bringing me.

"Then you retake it. All isn't lost. You can retake this thing over and over again, right? Like me with that shitty SAT? Goddamn verbal pissed me off."

I avoided his gaze as every bit of life and excitement rushed from me, pooling into a despondent puddle on the floor beneath my seat. All that studying. All those hours I'd given up doing something fun—doing *anything* I'd rather be doing. All that mental and emotional energy. I wasn't even sure if I could muster the courage to do it all again. Would I just get the same results?

"Yeah, I guess," I whispered.

He put a hand on my shoulder. "You know what? We're not going to think about this now. We're going to log on and blow shit up tonight."

I shrugged off his hand and shook my head. "I think I'm just going to take a nap."

"Mia—"

I held up my hand. "I'm sure you can pick up an enchanter or enchantress tonight for the group quest. Please? I just...I feel super gross right now and I'd like to be alone. Can you hit the Starbucks for their Internet?"

Heath looked at me for a long time. "Let me log in and cancel. I'll stay and hang out with you, make sure you're all right."

I pounded the desk in front of me. "I *am* all right, and I won't be able to crash if you're here. Please. I just need to be alone. I'll be okay. I promise."

Heath's forehead creases deepened. "Okay...how about I go down to the Starbucks in the Circle so I can look in on you on my way home?"

I shrugged. "If my light's off, don't knock. I'll be sleeping. It's about time I got some sleep. I'm just so exhausted. I'll call you in the morning." I hated the way my voice shook.

Heath's brows creased so close together they threatened to form a permanent unibrow, but he finally left.

And then... and then. Alice tumbled down the hole, ass over teakettle. And she didn't end up in Wonderland. Not even close. She wallowed, instead, marinated in the salt of her own tears and failure, in a stew of her own making. Haunted by *if only.*

If only I'd worked harder.

If only I'd stayed focused. What kind of a doctor would I make, after all, if I couldn't set aside personal worries and do the work I was trained for? What kind of doctor would I be if I got distracted when lives depended on me?

If only Mom hadn't gotten sick.

If only...

If only I hadn't lost hope.

I'd stayed in contact with Mom during all of this, calling her every day. Already she'd had four chemotherapy sessions, and I knew it wouldn't be long before it would take its toll. I'd managed to make it back home each weekend that I could scrape up the gas money—and the time—for the trip.

Whenever I talked to her, she sounded just a tiny bit more tired. Soon, her hair would fall out, if it hadn't started to already. Who knew what she wasn't telling me in attempt to protect me from the truth? So I wouldn't be distracted. So I'd succeed.

I couldn't even imagine the crushing disappointment she'd feel when she heard this news.

I hadn't just failed myself. I'd failed her.

And it hurt. It *hurt.* So damn much.

Maybe I wasn't good enough to be a doctor after all. This test was designed to weed out the wannabes from the meant-to-bes. Maybe I *was* a wannabe.

This thought more than any other left me sore, aching. Exhausted, I cried myself to sleep.

And since I had no class the next day, I slept in—well, I would have if my phone hadn't chimed at 8 a.m.

You okay? It was FallenOne.

I blinked sleep from my eyes and tried to process the message. Why had he texted me? Was he checking to find out why I hadn't logged on last night? Had Heath said something? How much should I tell FallenOne?

Hi. I'm fine, I replied.

His response came back in seconds. *I don't believe you.*

Why...because I'm such a hopeless addict that only the direst of circumstances would pull me away from logging in to DE? My sarcastic tendencies prevailed, even when emotionally exhausted and in a text message.

Something like that.

What did Fragged say to you guys?

He said you weren't feeling well. Is it okay to check up on a friend?

My thumbs hovered over the virtual keyboard, hesitating before I typed, *No, it's not. I'm fine.*

Again his response came back quickly. *So that's it? Just fine?*

I sighed, though he couldn't hear me. *You're being a pest. Haven't you got a class or something?*

Or something...but not for an hour. I have time. What's bugging you?

I got my MCAT results back...

My thumb hesitated over the 'send' button. Did I really want to go there with him? Was I prepared to dump this on a virtual-only friend? Then again, he was there for me when Mom got her diagnosis. Fallen had stayed up with me the entire night, proving that he cared.

I took a deep breath, hit the 'delete' button and retyped the message. *I bombed the MCAT.*

You have the results back already?

Yeah. Total fail.

Define "bombed," though. Does that mean you didn't get the score you were hoping for?

I bit the inside of my cheek as I continued to type, haunted again by what went wrong. Stress? Poor preparation? Who knew... *It means I'm an utter failure.*

Um. Not. I reject that statement utterly.

I'm afraid it's true.

No, Mia. So you got a shit score. You've had a lot going on in your life lately.

I'm afraid the AAMC doesn't accept excuse notes from my Mommy.

That's not what I meant. I meant you can retake it.

Until I figure out what went wrong, that'd probably be a mistake. But I might have to accept the fact that—I gulped out loud as I typed these next words—*I'll probably never be a doctor.*

Now you're just being silly. Of course you'll be a doctor. A damn good one. One who cares.

I need to figure out if that really is true, or if I'm just a wannabe who can't concentrate their way out of a paper bag enough to take a test.

That test is very hard, I've heard. I looked it up when you first told me about it. And you did have a lot going on. You can take it again. I've just Googled three different locations in the LA area that are giving it next month. I'll send you the link.

I suddenly realized that, not only was he trying to help, he was being incredibly sweet by attempting to cheer me up. And I was summarily pooping all over his little pep talk.

I bit my lip, thinking. I should probably back off the negativity. If I was being honest, he was making me feel a little better...

Thank you. I don't think I'll retake it again right away until I come up with a plan of attack. But when I do retake it, I'm definitely not driving to LA when it's given regularly in Anaheim and Fullerton. Much closer.

Seconds after hitting 'send,' it occurred to me that I'd just revealed my location. But after worrying for a split second, I shrugged it off. Over three million people lived in Orange County. It wasn't like he could stalk me from that info—even if he did decide to fly out to my side of the country and try to meet me, or something else weird.

TMI. I could be a serial killer, you know.

I laughed out loud and snorted through my nose. *I was starting to get that vibe from you, but after this test score I just got, I kinda have a death wish.*

I hope you are kidding. Please tell me you are kidding.

I was actually grinning now, despite feeling like shit. *I'm kidding.*

I have to go in a minute, but I'm checking on you later today. Please, will you call Fragged or me or someone if you are really feeling down?

My hands froze when I read that. Talk to him on the phone again? My stomach did a weird shivery butterfly type of thing. I'd been hoping, since our last call—despite the circumstances of it—that he'd try to call me again. *You have my word,* I replied.

You're logging on tonight, by the way. You and I will go do something fun. There's this cool spot in the Forgotten Ridge zone. A hidden cave. I'll show it to you.

My brow scrunched. Hidden cave? How would he know about something like that? *You're lying...I've never heard of that.*

It's top secret. Can't tell anyone. Can't blog about it.

I frowned even harder. *Why?*

Cuz then it wouldn't be secret anymore!

If it's so secret, how did you find out about it? And why tell me... a blogger?

I could tell you, but then I'd have to kill you.

*So you*are a serial killer.*

I am a serial killer...of pixelated goblins, trolls and vampires. And all that other shit we have to grind on to level up.

I sighed and sat back, surprised that in the past few minutes, I'd almost forgotten to be miserable.

So you're logging on, right?

Or else what?

Or else I'll tell Fragged to go over there and bother you.

I'll log on. Besides, if he comes over here, his BF will have a tantrum. Tonight's their date night.

Great. It's just you and me then. And our secret little hideaway.

I almost—*almost*—typed *"It's a date"* before I thought better of it.

***

Fallen did take me on an adventure, as promised. We met near the transport station and climbed aboard a gondola borne inside the claws of a huge silver dragon. It worked much like a blimp, fantasy-style, carrying us across the continent with the persistent flapping of giant, fabled reptilian wings instead of the laws of thermodynamics. In the game, these long journeys were represented by real-time delays.

It was during one of these delays, somewhere between the Ancient City's Dragon Tower and our unknown destination, high above the Forgotten Ridge Mountains, that Fallen messaged me.

*FallenOne tells you, *Click on the trap door. Now!*

Trap door? My eyes raced across the screen until they landed on the bottom level of the gondola, where there was, in fact, a small trap door tucked away in the corner. I immediately did as he said. Suddenly, my character was free-falling beside his, a fall that under normal circumstances would lead to certain death. Obviously, there was nothing normal about this place.

We plunged into an isolated mountain lake nestled among the mountaintops. From the bottom of the zone and traveling on foot—or even on a mount—this area, I knew, was inaccessible.

I knew because I'd tried to climb to the tops of these mountains once, and the game had not allowed it. I'd reached the "edge" of what was reachable by players. Somehow, FallenOne had discovered a "hole" in that barrier by dropping through from above...and he was rewarded with this beautiful place.

The sun was just coming up over the jagged ridge, the virtual sky the color of peaches and cream. Our characters were treading water in the lake, the swoosh, swoosh of the water rippling around us. I could have stayed right there forever, but FallenOne directed us toward one particular edge that faced a cliff.

We swam across the lake toward that edge, where a tall, forceful waterfall fell into the lake with big splashes, its powerful ripples moving outward.

*FallenOne tells you, *When you swim through the waterfall, dive downward. At the bottom of the lake, you'll see an entrance—swim into it. You have to do this pretty quickly or you'll end up running out of breath and drowning. Ready?*

A hidden entrance to a cave, behind a waterfall, in a lake that is otherwise inaccessible to players unless they knew about the hole in the flyover zone?

Talk about well hidden!

Too damn bad I couldn't write about this on my blog...

I followed FallenOne's instructions, ending up in a tiny underwater tunnel at the bottom of the lake. We were almost out of breath when the tunnel curved upward and we surfaced in a fantasy-type of fairy grotto.

Holy crap! I typed. *This is incredible...*

Watery light trickled in from an indirect source, and something on the walls of the cave gave off a bright green, bioluminescent glow. There were jewel-colored stalagmites hanging from the ceiling, their matching stalactites reaching up from the ground. The water was crystal clear, the surface reflecting everything, and the distant, melodic sound of water dripped in a steady rhythm. It was stunning.

From where we stood in the shallow water of the cave pool, it appeared as if the cave had rooms that led off into other passageways.

Me: *This place is huge. It looks like it goes on and on.*
Him: *Wanna explore?*
Me: *Do I? Does a mynock love to chew on power cords?*

We found a room that had furniture in it—rustic style, carved from raw timbers and tied with animal skins. Another room had initials carved into the stone in the wall. Sometimes just two initials like A.D. or C.W., and sometimes three, like J.G.F. or W.J.D. It was virtual graffiti. Everyone's initials were carved in a different style of writing, as if they had been scrawled there by the people themselves.

Who were they? Game developers? Employees of the company that created DE? Family and friends of the developer who had tucked this cave down here?

How incredibly strange…and wonderful.

We continued our exploration. Part of the cave opened out into a hidden meadow behind the mountain. It was full of wildflowers and a crisp, blue sky sparkling with the newly risen sun. *Beautiful.*

Me: *I wish a paradise like this existed in real life.*
Him: *Feel better now?*
Me: *Yes! Thank you.*
Him: *You're welcome.*
Me: *Now are you going to tell me how you knew about this place?*

Him: *Let's just say I've spent some time exploring and looking for loopholes.*

Me: *Who ARE you? How do you have time to do that?*

I might have suspected him of being an employee of the company that designed the game, except that I knew the company was California-based and he most decidedly kept East Coast hours. Maybe he had a friend who worked for the company...

Knowing FallenOne—well, what little I *did* know—these things would likely remain a mystery for years to come. And I could accept that or try to badger the truth out of him.

I chose to accept it.

***

It took about a week, but eventually I recovered from the great MCAT disaster of the decade. Not that the stinging sense of failure completely went away.

I mostly bounced back due to Heath coming over to physically drag me out to the movies, miniature golf or just wherever. And Kat and FallenOne's virtual nagging to log on and grind quests with them. We got Kat her complete heal spell and moved on to Fragged's barbarian quest to learn hidden techniques from the Great Mercenary Hermit—who, ironically, lived in the Forgotten Ridge.

FallenOne never hinted to the others about the hidden cave, and as much as I would have liked to, I kept mum also. Thus it would remain our little secret hidey-hole, an almost unbelievable virtual paradise. But I never went back, either.

One night, a few weeks later, we were working on Heath's incredibly tedious quest—with much good-natured bitching from both Persephone and me.

"Stop complaining, Eloisa. Your big quest is next. Unless you want me to moan and groan the entire time we work on it," Heath said. "Payback is a bitch."

"And so are you," I replied back to him in a split second.

A skilled mercenary was a bonus to everyone in the group, since he was the one who stood up front, shouting annoying things at the monsters so they'd only attack him. His sole job was to stand there like a meat shield and get beaten on while the rest of us took the mob down. At this level, every fight was a team effort.

"You know," I said after we'd killed our fifteenth troll. "I'm enjoying this game a lot. There's something for everyone, and I like the creativity of the quests. I just wish they had something for those of us who want to dig deeper and solve a mystery." My thoughts kept circling back to that hidden cave and why it was there. I'd wanted to dig deeper.

FallenOne sent a message to the group, *What do you mean?*

"Well, for example, I'd love it if there was a secret quest." I straightened in my chair and watched the monitor, hitting the appropriate buttons for my spells as they lit up the screen like a thunderstorm. "Like something hidden in the game beneath the obvious quests. Maybe we'd have to look for clues or speak to NPCs to get hints that lead us on secret quest chains. I love being forced to think outside the box."

That's a really interesting idea, FallenOne commented.

"Well, someday there will be a game that will do stuff like that," I said.

Fragged laughed. "I don't even think they *could* do something like that. Not with current programming technology."

I hit my last nuke spell to finish off the big monster, then indicated that we needed to wait until my mana regenerated before our next fight. "I wish they could. Dragon Epoch is so much more advanced than the MMOs I've played up 'til now. If anyone could do something cool like that, it would be the people who made DE."

"Maybe," Fragged replied.

FallenOne chimed in, *It wouldn't be hard to implement. Some creatively constructed nested coding.*

Fragged snorted. "Oh, so now you're an expert at coding, are you?" Not that we had any idea what he *was* an expert at...except for keeping secrets.

FallenOne said to the group, */shrug It's just a guess. Maybe it would be too hard. Who knows?*

I sighed. "That would be a shame if it is, because it could be a lot of fun. Like, they could drop weekly hints to the players who are interested. I dunno. It was just a thought."

Hints? That's weak sauce. Make the players work for it, said Fallen.

"Well, however they wanted to do it," I replied. "They could get all creative, even have it open a new zone or expansion. It would have a whole story behind it."

"Anyway," Persephone interrupted. "Aren't we supposed to be finding this named boss to finish Fragged's quest?"

"He hasn't spawned yet," said Fragged.

Persephone sighed. "Let's go do something else for a little while. I'm bored." A common complaint coming from our energetic Canadian friend.

"You're bloodthirsty," Fragged accused.

And they continued a good-natured argument while another conversation started.

*FallenOne tells you, *So tell me more about this secret quest idea. I think it's cool.*

I smiled, bit my bottom lip and replied.

*You tell FallenOne, *Oh, it's just an off the cuff idea. I would love it if the game put in hidden surprises like that. Easter eggs, you know? Just fun little secret quests for us to discover when we get bored collecting Giant Lizard tongues for the random local witch or tiger teeth for the shaman in town...*

Him: *Those quests aren't *that bad...*

Me: *No, they're not bad, but they don't exactly make you think outside of the box, know what I mean? It just seems to me that DE is such a kickass game, and they've shown with their game design that they are awesome. I think it would be a fun idea if they could implement it. Too bad they don't have a "suggestion box" so that players can submit ideas like that to the designers.*

Him: *Haha, very funny. Hopefully, you're actually using the suggestion box instead of being snarktastic. Or maybe they should just read your blog. Someone should tell them about it.*

Me: *Someone already did, apparently. I've been linked on the landing page of their website several times, shockingly enough!*

Him: *You downplay how good your blog is. You shouldn't do that.*

Me: *Well... thanks. I'm glad you like it. If I don't end up being a doctor, maybe I can figure out how to live off my leet blogging skillz.*

"What the hell are you two doing, smoking ganja?" Fragged yelled over the headset. "We're fighting here!"

That was the end of that. We finished Fragged's quest that night. And later, I actually submitted the damn secret quest idea to the suggestion box that probably no one ever checked.

If they did, who knew if the idea would take hold or not? But it sure would be cool if it did.

Chapter 8:
Truth or Dare

FALL ROLLED AROUND AGAIN, AND WITH IT, THE START of my senior year—my last semester of coursework with several of the most challenging classes I'd taken in my entire college career. As for the MCAT, I'd spent a good two months re-evaluating what had gone wrong and come up with a plan of attack.

Clearly, there was a whole strategy behind taking the test. I had to learn that strategy. And quick.

Because the longer I delayed retaking it, the more it would delay my med school applications. I risked losing an entire year between finishing college and moving on to medical school.

I sucked it up and joined a study group. *So* not my thing, and yet annoyingly necessary.

"Maybe we should start with some introductions?" the perky blonde started, shifting on her chair in one of the reserved study rooms in the Chapman University Leatherby Libraries. "I'm Alicia Smiley, majoring in Organic Chem. No jokes about the name, please and thank you. I do smile a lot." She punctuated that statement with perfect matching dimples on each cheek.

The small group laughed at her little joke. We'd used a university forum to match up, based on the approximate date we'd be taking the MCAT test. Most of them were a year behind me in school, and I planned on keeping mum about my previous failure.

Next to introduce himself was a guy with straggly dark hair plastered to his forehead and an ugly sweater. He quietly introduced himself as Clark. I mentally reframed him as wearing glasses a la Clark Kent. The next image came to my mind was of him ripping off that atrocious sweater to reveal a blue body suit with a giant 'S' on his chest. I had to bite my lip to stifle the giggles.

A few others introduced themselves. Then it was my turn. "I'm Mia Strong. Bio major. And, um, yeah, I just want to do really well on this test." That rock in my stomach twisted again, like it did every time I contemplated my failure and what it might mean if I didn't get off my ass and pass this damn test.

Lastly, a really young-looking guy with curly blond hair and boy-next-door good looks leaned forward. "I'm Jon. Kinesiology major. I'm a recent transfer from Penn—as in the Ivy League University of Pennsylvania, *not* Penn State. And I will cut a person who confuses the two. JK of course."

Nervous laughter all around. Anyone from the west coast had little idea what the difference was between those two schools—besides the fact that one was Ivy League and the other had a famous football team. Nor did we care. Harvard or Stanford, we understood. The Penns? Not so much.

I laughed along with the rest of the group, and when Jon's gaze landed on me, a cocky smile appeared. I smiled back and something in his eyes changed, intensifying. Like headlights being switched onto high beam, I drew back.

Uh oh. I'd seen that look before, when I'd bothered to look back long enough to notice.

I immediately averted my gaze and made a point to ignore Jon the rest of the study session. Before leaving, we passed around a sheet, sharing phone numbers and email addresses, then set up another meeting. Miss Smiley McDimples—as I was now mentally calling her—would send us an agenda based on the specs of the test within the next few days, and we'd come back to the group, prepared to pair off and quiz each other.

I could do this. I got this. I chanted these phrases to myself as I rushed out of the room the minute we were done. As a protective measure, I pressed my cell phone to my ear, pretending to talk on it lest anyone think they could approach me afterward.

I'd learned a lot of tricks like that, and they worked really well. Some would say too well.

"When *are* you going to start dating, anyway?" Heath had asked me recently.

"The 12th of Never in the year of our Lord, hypothetically speaking."

Heath sighed and rolled his eyes. "Stubborn girl."

"*Determined* girl." I quirked a brow, folding my arms across my chest. "My life is not going to depend on the whims of some man."

Heath grinned. "Believe me, the whims of some man can be very pleasurable… when you find the right man."

"And have *you* found him, Heath?" When the smile dropped abruptly from his face, I knew I'd said the wrong thing. *Oh shit.* I was always saying the wrong thing lately. "I mean, as long as he makes you happy, right?"

After an awkward pause, the subject was changed and I made a mental note to handle that topic much more smoothly in the future. Although prickly responses like that served me well because they taught Heath to avoid the subject from then on. And he was a quick learner, fortunately.

Mom, well, she was another story. But usually she didn't push it. She just looked at me with sad eyes, and I knew she was thinking about what had happened to me in high school. Whenever she brought up the subject, however, I managed to change it. That was that.

***

As this was my last year at the university, the pressure was piling on. My days consisted of classes, homework for aforementioned classes, extra work for the MCAT study group, research at the lab for—and sometimes with—my advising professor. Hours at the hospital, though they were reduced again, now that summer was over. And, when I could fit them in, blogging and gaming. Sleeping and eating were sandwiched somewhere in between. Rinse and repeat.

Sadly, our gaming group only got together one night a week, but I managed a few more hours here and there when I could. And when I did, I frequently ran into FallenOne. I often wondered if that was by accident or by design.

But why question a good thing, right?

Of course, Kat's suspicions swirled around in my mind as well. Did FallenOne like me?

I had to admit...I kind of liked him.

*FallenOne tells you, *I've been thinking about that secret quest thingy you were talking about a few weeks ago. It's a cool idea.*

*You tell FallenOne, *They could be already working on something like that. I wouldn't be surprised.*

Him: *Neither would I.*

Me: *Yeah, when these geeky dudes aren't totally obsessing about women's bodies, they are pretty smart.*

Him: *So you think all us geeky types just obsess over women?*

Me: *Am I wrong?*

Him: *How is that different than any other guy, though?*

Me: *Good point. Probably not different. Unless you're Heath.*

***

It only took two more study sessions for Jon to ask me out. It was simply for coffee afterward and "just to get some extra study time in." Also, it had been after we'd been randomly—or so I'd hoped—paired up during the second session to quiz each other, and he'd deliberately sat next to me in the third.

I hated having to shoot someone down. Especially someone as nice as Jon. And deep down, I asked myself, would it really be *that* unpleasant if I did go out to coffee with him?

But coffee would lead to drinks. And drinks might lead to going out to a club or dancing or whatever normal people my age did. And then that might lead to "swing by my place afterward." And then...and then. That was the part that always brought me to a halt.

"I'm sorry. I'm super busy. Meeting a friend in an hour."

"Okay..." He drew that out, expecting me, perhaps, to fill in the knowledge gap. When I wasn't forthcoming, he changed tactics. "Oh. I guess I should have asked if you had a boyfriend."

"I don't..." His expression visibly brightened. Maybe I should have lied instead? "*But,* I'm very serious about my studies. I'm on a scholarship, which requires perfect grades. I don't do much of anything, including dating."

His eyebrows rose. "Oh. Are you religious?" It was a fair question. Chapman University was a church-related school, after all, and there were quite a few people who attended it based on that affiliation. But not me. I attended based on the nice, fat, full-ride scholarship they'd offered me when I finished high school.

Again, I could have lied about that, but chose not to. "Not particularly, no. It's just a personal choice."

Jon blinked, confused, and I gathered my things, ready to shake him off. He followed as I rushed out the door of the library as if I had places to go, things to do, people to see. I *did* have a lot to do that day—okay, maybe not a *lot,* but there was a project to finish and laundry to squeeze in there somewhere.

I guess 'personal choice' was not an acceptable excuse, because Jon made a good-natured remark about "wearing me down." I, just as good-naturedly, joked that there were several eligible members of our group—Smiley McDimples, for one— who had seemed interested in him.

Jon was not dissuaded, if the determined look in his eyes was any indication.

Nevertheless, I was able to deter him and continue about my day. Unfortunately, my evening would, in a sense, prove to be more of the same.

While gaming with my friends, I took breaks to run down and change clothes from the washer to the dryer. Proof I wasn't lying!

Tonight, it was FallenOne's turn, so we worked on his epic weapon quest, the Staff of Mighty Power. For one of the components, we needed a very special feather from a very rare creature. The Surperfluous Flamingo spawned in the Lost Lagoon. But we had to hack through hordes of hostile hippos, rabid gators, and aggro ostriches by the thousands, killing placeholders over and over again in order to get it to spawn. It took *hours.*

Long, boring hours. To the point where we were starting to break out the caffeinated drinks and get a little punchy, making jokes and laughing at every little thing.

Fallen had long since offered to give up, but we wouldn't allow it. We were the stubbornest bunch of ornery mofos on the server, and we weren't going to give in.

We were going to snatch that rare feather off that fucking flamingo if it was the last thing we did!

It was a hot night in late September, the worst month for heat in Southern California. My studio apartment—as fortuitous a find as it was—lacked air conditioning, and thus I had to rely on box fans in the windows for some relief. It did very little beyond blowing hot air all over me.

Of course, open windows meant I had a direct line to the screeching and howling of my neighbors, who enjoyed loud, raucous sex at any temperature. Warm, cold, hot, dry. Rain or shine. Those two screwed like dogs in perpetual heat.

"God dammit. The neighbors are going at it again," I finally said after the fourth "Oh God!" in a row.

Kat sighed heavily. "I wish *I* was having sex right now. I'm jealous."

"Who doesn't?" replied Heath.

"That doesn't mean I'd rather hear my neighbors going on and on about it. *Damn.* Someone needs to introduce them to online gaming or something."

"Yeah, because camping a rare spawn is *so* much more fun than orgasms," replied Heath.

"Maybe we should do something to pass the time while we do this shitty camp. Obviously not as fun as what Mia's neighbors are doing...but how about a game? Truth or dare, anyone?" asked Persephone.

"What the hell are you going to dare us to do? Streak through the swamp with no armor on? Can I get a 'hell no'?" Heath replied.

"Ah, c'mon," Kat whined. "I'll go first. What's the craziest place you've had sex? Truth, you have to answer. Dare, you have to fight the next mob solo with no weapon while we all stand back and laugh at you."

"That's an easy one," Heath replied. "Under the bleachers at my high school during a basketball game."

"What?" I gasped. "Heath? Not even."

He laughed. "It is, indeed, true."

I scoffed. "With who?"

"Ah, ah, ah! No cheating," Kat admonished. "It's not your turn to ask. Fallen, how do you choose? Answer the question, or do you drop your nunchakus and solo the mob with your fists?"

As usual, Fallen responded via text only. But since he typed so fast, it was easy for him to keep up with us.

Oh, hell. Why not? Truth. Mine is from high school, too. I worked at my uncle's office my junior year and got propositioned by this chick who also worked there. We did it on the conference table after-hours when no one else was around.

"Oh dayum!" Heath roared, laughing. "Yours is better than mine."

Hell no, there wasn't a crowd around for mine! Fallen shot back.

"No, but I bet that made the next conference meeting…interesting. Especially with your uncle sitting there."

*Nope, I just moved boxes around and took care of mail at that job. I never had to sit at in at conference meetings. *She had to, though, so I assume it was awkward for her LOL.*

"Huh. Well, I'm sure there was a lot of *poking* and *prodding* during those special conference meetings," Kat said.

Just that one time there, anyway. We got more conventional later on.

Once our teasing died down, Katya spoke again. "Okay, Mia. Spill… or are you soloing with no magic?"

"No magic?! Wait!" I panicked, suddenly having to rearrange my plan, which had been to choose "dare" and burn the mob down with my biggest one-thumper of a nuke spell. I'd been saving it, because the refresh time on the spell made it so I could only cast it once every twenty minutes. "You said no weapon. I won't use my wand."

"Magic *is* your weapon. So given these mobs spawning, I'm going to say that squishy little you will last one, maybe two hits before you go down."

"Just spill the goods, Mia," Heath said.

Fragged tells you, It's not like you really have a lot to tell, anyway, right?

You tell Fragged, Thanks for your support, champ. I'll remember this.

I also remembered that I didn't have anything to be ashamed of. "Fine, then. Truth. I don't have a weird place."

"So you've only ever done it in a bed?" Kat asked, disbelief in her voice.

"I've never done it at all," I replied, folding my arms over my chest, though I knew they couldn't see me.

FallenOne commented, *Wait, what?*

"No way," Kat said. "I don't believe you."

"Heath can verify. I don't date. I don't hook up..."

"Are you religious?" Kat asked. Wow...second time today that question had been asked.

"Nope. Just haven't had the desire." That wasn't exactly true. I'd just had a bad experience...one I had *no* desire to talk about. So, I let that stand.

"I can verify," Heath interjected. "She's a virgin...as far as I know. I mean, we've been friends since we were thirteen and all. On the other hand, she had no idea about my escapade at the basketball game—which I think she even attended. So take my verification for what it's worth. Though I stand as witness to the fact that she doesn't date."

And yet you make fun of all the nerdy game designers who you say can't get any? Fallen asked.

"There's a difference between wanting it and not getting it, and not wanting it in the first place. But mostly, that's all joking on my part. It's just me being grouchy about all the female skin they think it's necessary to show."

Kat asked, "Are you a prude, Mia? Or are you just saving yourself for marriage?"

I sat back with a sigh. Those labels again. Why did there always have to be labels for a woman's sexual status? *Prude. Tease. Slut.* They reflected an entire spectrum that described levels of access to a female's body by any given man.

"'Prude' is a rude word to use. And I don't plan on getting married, so that eliminates my saving myself for something that will never happen. But why try to label me based on my sexual status? Why do there always have to be labels instead of respecting personal choices?"

There was a pause, and I could tell that they were all thinking about what I'd said. Finally, Kat cleared her throat. "Yeah, you're right. 'Prude' is as bad as 'slut.' I didn't mean it in a mean way, and I'm sorry. Maybe you can reclaim it and make it yours. Like…I know I'm a slut and I'm not ashamed of it."

"Maybe, but prude has such a negative connotation. Like if you don't have sex, you must not like it. How do I know if I like it or not? I've never had it!"

Good point, agreed FallenOne.

"So maybe I'll pick a new label for myself. I'm 'cheerfully celibate.'"

"There's a lot to be said for choosing not to get wrapped up in all the baggage that sex can bring," Kat said, her voice much more serious now. "I was *way* too young when I started."

"Me, too," Heath concurred.

I shook my head. "Seriously, *when* was all this happening? I had no idea."

Heath's dry laugh sounded in my headset. "When you're a gay teen, you get to be an expert at keeping secrets—at least until you come out of the closet. Then you're ready to trumpet it to the world!"

"And march naked in gay pride parades?" asked Kat.

Heath laughed. "Or just sit by the sidelines and thoroughly enjoy them!"

"Well, now you all know my sordid secret," I said.

Nothing sordid or shameful about it. Actually, it's pretty awesome. Good for you, Mia, FallenOne pitched in.

I smiled and then breathed a sigh of relief. I no longer regretted my candor. Not a single "you don't know what you're missing," like I'd expected. Well…good.

So I was still a virgin… so what? Maybe I'd die an old lady virgin, or maybe I'd try it out once to see what all the fuss was about. But whatever I decided, the decision was mine.

Chapter 9:
Aim to Misbehave

IN SPITE OF MY VANISHING SPARE TIME, I MADE AN EFFORT to get home to see Mom at least once every two weeks—even if only part of a day. Sometimes my work schedule wasn't cooperative, though. More than once I traded for a graveyard shift on a Thursday night, went straight to morning class on Friday and then caught a catnap for a few hours before hitting the road.

Since Mom lived in a remote area that was not accessible by train or bus, driving was the only option. I still managed to get some studying in though, even during the drive. A person in my study group turned me on to a free MCAT strategy podcast, and I listened as I drove to absorb more tips on how to pass that damn test.

On a gorgeous Saturday morning, we drove to the Idyllwild farmers market to buy produce. Mom wanted to show me how to make the old family baklava recipe, determined that only the best ingredients would do.

I couldn't bring myself to ask if this was some kind of frantic handing down of inherited knowledge. Her mom had taught her how to make this same dessert, so I tried to look at this like a natural rite of passage as the next female in line. But my hands shook as I minced the walnuts and pistachios according to her directions. Would this be her last chance to show me? What if she didn't get better?

"You need to stop throwing me those looks. I'm starting to get self-conscious," she said without looking at me.

Guiltily, I returned my attention to the chopping board. "What looks? Don't know what you're talking about. You look great."

She gave me a thin smile. "I *do* look great, if I do say so myself. And I think I could have pulled one over on you... maybe even never told you what was going on. I think a nasty flu would have explained a few bad days, and you would have been none the wiser."

I frowned and carefully set down my knife. "What do you mean 'pull one over' on me? You mean, not tell me that you were sick?"

She shrugged. "I could have waited 'til I was all better to spill the beans. I don't like how you've been worrying. How you've been breaking your back to come home as often as you have. Though... gotta say I love seeing you so much."

I made a face at her. "As if you could have hidden that from me."

She bit her bottom lip and an expression clouded her eyes—something a bit like...guilt? Was there something she wasn't telling me? Faint suspicions I'd been harboring all weekend were on high alert. "You *are* all right, aren't you? The doctor says you're getting better?"

Her bottom lip escaped her teeth, and she moved closer to me, cupping my cheek with her hand. "I am. I promise. You know as much as I do."

I let out a sigh as she pointed to the chopping board. "That has to be a lot finer if you want the baklava to turn out half decent."

Grumbling, I picked up the knife and returned to my task, trying very hard not to dart any more concerned glances her way.

This continued until it was time to leave on Sunday afternoon. On my way out, I cast a cursory glance at my mom's desk as I landed a kiss on her papery cheek. Mom had taken to wearing scarves—to hide her bald head—underneath her straw cowboy hat, paired with big sunglasses. A look somewhere between a faded Hollywood starlet and a well-worn cowgirl.

During my drive home, however, that niggling suspicion finally hit me over the head like a baseball bat. On Mom's desk, I'd seen multiple bills stacked up—unopened. I *knew* they were bills because they had the little window envelopes; plus, she immediately shredded junk mail when she received it. If she'd kept and stacked those envelopes, they were important.

I made a mental note to broach the subject with her during our next phone call. She *had* temporarily shut down the B&B to deal with her health crisis. And I'd been glad of that, as it eased her work burden while she healed. But with no money coming in…how was she paying her regular bills, and on top of that, her medical bills?

These concerns combined with others…I worried about her, all alone up there. I was her only backup at this point. I had to keep an eye out for her.

As I continued to drive, my mind drifted toward the week ahead, a weary exhaustion engulfing me with the thought of beginning the vicious cycle once more. More days of classes, homework, meticulous medical research, working the hospital job, studying for the MCAT retake….

I felt like I was on a neverending hamster wheel, and slowly but surely, it was grinding me down.

I looked forward, with everything that was in me, to our weekly gaming night. Thank God for my online friends.

But even immersion in my favorite game with some of my favorite people was not enough to tear me fully away from all the worries.

Case in point, we were fighting in a huge frozen cavern full of Ice Giants. They'd stomp and drop boulders on us while we chopped at their ankles and slowly brought them down. I usually loved fighting giants because I could use my magic to charm them to fight for me. If the spell worked, a giant under my control would turn on his fellow giants and act as my pet gigantic assassin. For me, fighting giants was a treat.

This time it wasn't. Usually I could keep three busy by mesmerizing one and charming another to fight the third while my group members attacked the fourth without impediment.

Except I screwed up the order I was supposed to do things, and the giant I was trying to charm instead started to pound me into goo. Once I was no longer keeping the three extraneous giants occupied, they turned on my party members, making guacamole out of them as well.

Such was life. We wiped.

And subsequently, we reappeared as ghosts at our bind point.

Through my headset, I could hear Heath furiously clicking on his keyboard—as if sending messages to the others that he didn't want me to see. "Guys, this is our third wipe in the

Mammoth Ice Caverns. I'm not feeling it tonight. Want to go do something a little easier? We can get back to this next week."

"Sounds good to me," agreed Kat without any argument whatsoever. No acknowledgement of my mistakes. No reprimand. I loved my friends.

*FallenOne tells you, *You've been quiet lately.*

In spite of my distracted state, I always got a little thrill whenever FallenOne private messaged me first. I leaned forward to reply.

*You tell FallenOne, *Sorry. Preoccupied.*
Him: *How's your mom?*
Me: *Getting better. I think. Won't know for sure until she goes in to get a scan in a few months.*
Him: *I'm sure she'll be okay.*
Me: *My research professor tries to reassure me, too. He's an oncologist, so I guess he knows WTF he's talking about. But it's one thing to know something in your head and a different thing to feel that fear in your heart, know what I mean?*
Him: *Sure. Yes. I definitely do.*
Me: *I've decided I want to be an oncologist. Cancer needs its ass kicked—badly.*
Him: *That's awesome... not only because you've decided to choose that in honor of your mom, but that you know what you want to do at such a young age. What are you, 20? 21?*

Me: *Are you actually asking me personal questions while telling me nothing about yourself? I ask your a/s/l and you just answer that you're a dude. I don't even know if THAT is true.*

Except I *did*. I'd heard his voice on the phone. For a few garbled minutes, anyway. A few minutes which had sparked my curiosity for more. But he'd never offered to call again, and my pride may have been too bruised to ask him for another phone call. I wanted him to offer it. Though I got the feeling, given his pervasive reluctance to divulge details about himself, Fallen was studiously avoiding the subject of another phone call.

I sat back with a sigh and waited, ignoring the fight on the screen as I stared at the blinking cursor in the dialogue box, wondering how he'd answer. Would he finally come clean or evade, like usual? I had to admit that I was intensely curious about him and became more curious as days went by—which only meant that he became much stingier with his info. And, of course, I began to wonder if he was playing a game within the game.

Him: *I practice cyber safety. *Strict cyber safety.*

Me: *So you're afraid I'm going to find you, stalk you and boil your pet rabbit?*

Him: *Never had a pet rabbit, fortunately. And anonymity is a gift. It's hard to give up—sometimes so hard that it's almost impossible, even when you want to. I guess it's kind of like burrowing yourself into a cozy little hole and not wanting the gig to be up.*

Me: *Now it's sounding like YOU are the rabbit.*

Him: *I'm sorry, I don't mean to be difficult. I just think it's better this way.*

My mouth quirked when I read that line. That meant he was married or had a girlfriend. *Definitely* a girlfriend, at the very least. Perhaps he'd been understating the matter in true male fashion when he'd mentioned his date was "just a friend." Who knew? *And why did I care?*

He was just a friend, right? Like Heath? And Kat? And what I hoped Alex and Jenna might become someday? Someone I could depend upon—and could depend on me in turn.

But how could I ever become close friends with someone I knew next to nothing about? Was that even possible? And did I really want a friend like that?

We wiped again, and Heath called it a night with a frustrated sigh. My shoulders slumped, knowing I'd let everyone down. Katya made her excuses soon after, and then it was just Fallen and me, grinding away on *dailies*—repeatable quests that gave us experience and some other benefits.

It also gave us a chance to continue our previous chat.

Me: *If anonymity is a gift, then maybe I should practice some too.*
Him: *Fair enough. I can respect that.*
Me: *You pretty much have to...*

I tapped my fingers over my palmed mouse, waiting for his comeback. It never came. He changed the subject instead!

Him: *So let me ask you this...why do you want to be a doctor?*
Me: *Whoa, that wasn't even a subtle sidestep.*
Him: *Sorry. I just figured that we had said all that needed to be said on the subject. Don't you?*
Me: *Hmm. I suppose. But we're back to personal questions again.*

Him: *Not identifying questions, though...*
Me: *I guess so... I've always wanted to be a doctor to help people.*
Him: *That's cool. I admire that.*
Me: *How about you? Do you know what you want to do?*

Or maybe he was already doing what he wanted to do. That question assumed he was still young enough to be deciding his future. Maybe being a middle-aged basement-dwelling mailman was indeed his lifelong dream!

Him: *More or less. I'm of the same mind as you. I want to help people too, but in a different way. By entertaining them. Or giving them a way to escape.*

God, I hope that meant he was an actor-wannabe and not some paid escort, which is what it sounded like. But hey, escorts made a lot of money so...whatever worked for him. I couldn't stop giggling at the thought: *FallenOne, College Gigolo.*

Him: *It's getting late...I should probably go. And so should you. After all, you have to take on the world, right?*
Me: *That's me, world changer!*
Him: *Tell me you're going to re-register for the MCAT next month.*
Me: *I'll think about it.*

This same little routine seemed to repeat itself at the end of all of our gaming sessions—Fallen nagging me to register for a test retake, me pushing back due to fear.

It was endearing. And...sweet. And frustrating, because he was still holding back. Katya had told me she thought he'd come around eventually. That he was just shy. But I figured *my* guess was probably more accurate...

He was hiding a big secret. I had no idea what it was, but pondering this mystery was making me tired, to be honest.

I needed friends. Friends who *didn't* hold back. Friends whom I could count on in the *real* world for support. I vowed to hang out with Alex and Jenna more—when I could fit it in— and say "yes" to whatever they proposed next.

I just prayed that it wasn't some crazy college antics, or a frat party or something...

***

Weeks later, I got that chance on a rare night off. And fortunately, it wasn't a frat party. Instead of gaming, I hung out with Jenna and Alex at their off-campus apartment in Fullerton.

It was late. *Late* late. I should've been on my way home, but I sat hunched in their dark living room in front of their aging TV—a big fat CRT that Alex inherited when her mom upgraded to a flat screen. The popcorn bowl had long since transformed into a greasy vessel of congealed melted butter, salt and a billion unpopped kernels.

Through the holes in my sweater—while hiding the fact that I was trying to hide— I watched the "Bushwhacked" episode of *Firefly* with Alex and Jenna. The crew of *Serenity* had discovered a derelict ship floating in space with no known survivors aboard. And, knowing nothing of what had occurred on the ship, they searched it for loot and to hopefully discover what happened.

I'd seen the episode before—several times. As a devoted *Firefly* fan, I had about a dozen episodes from the short-lived but beloved TV series to choose from. I may have seen this particular one a dozen times, but it got me *every time*.

"Oh shit, I hate anything to do with the Reavers," Alex breathed. "They scare the crap out of me." She shifted a big cushion in front of her face then occasionally peeked around it at the screen.

The only one of us who appeared unaffected by the onscreen tension was Jenna, who sat with her legs crossed, her elbows resting on her knees, her chin in her hands, staring at the screen. "They're gonna *get* you, Alex! The cannibalistic space pirates are going to sneak into your room tonight!"

"Shut up, Jenna."

Jenna only snickered in response and then repeated Zoë's famous quote about the villainous Reavers. "They'll rape you to death, eat your flesh and sew your skin into their clothing. And if you're very, very *lucky,* they'll do it in that order."

I shuddered just as, onscreen, Jayne was hit from behind. Wildly pivoting, he started shooting. Alex and I both jumped when he was hit while Jenna continued smiling as if watching a leprechaun riding a unicorn over a rainbow. Honestly, that girl had either seen this episode eight thousand times—a definite possibility—or had nerves of titanium, possibly both.

Suddenly, we were startled by four figures who burst through the apartment door in the dark, shouting gutturally. We all jumped out of our seats and ran for the adjacent kitchen while the guys chased us wearing Halloween horror masks. My heart raced, the adrenaline pumping. Flailing about randomly with her hands, Alex emitted high-pitched screams. The more she shrieked, the more deep, harsh laughter came from the masked invaders. Even Jenna had let out a scream when they first entered. But now she was standing in the kitchen with her arms folded across her chest.

"Okay, douchebags," she finally said. "Very funny."

"Made ya scream, Jen. That's one of a hundred that we owe you."

"Bite me, Orin," she sneered, kicking a leg in the direction of his crotch. If he'd been standing closer, he'd have been the one letting loose a high-pitched scream. Even three feet away, he stepped back, yanking off his mask.

"Assholes!" Alex screamed again. "I'm so getting you back for that."

"Hey, that was for the glitter-bombing! We're even now," one of them replied. Alex had told me about that prank. The girls had loaded up a box and labeled it "baked goods," when it was actually a balloon-powered package of glitter explosions waiting to happen. "We're still finding glitter all over the place. That was effin' mean."

"Crybabies," Jenna replied. "Maybe you should clean your filthy pit once in a while, and the glitter would be gone."

"Why don't *you* clean it? Isn't that what women are supposed to do anyway?"

Wisely, they delivered that line while running out the door. Jenna chased them to the stairwell, cackling all the way, and they noticeably increased their speed. Smart of them. She would have kicked their asses—literally—if she'd caught them.

She returned, breathing hard, as Alex and I were picking up the overturned bowl of popcorn kernels that Alex had launched at the intruders when they'd busted through the door.

"Okay, we start our plans of revenge *tonight*," Jenna muttered through clenched teeth.

"Aren't you afraid it'll only escalate the conflict?" I picked popcorn crumbs from the outdated shag carpeting and glanced from one to the other.

"A girl can't back down," Alex mumbled before leaving the room and quickly returning, lugging the vacuum. "Otherwise, they'll keep terrorizing us. Speaking of which, lock the door in case they decide to come back. We need like a password or something."

"Yeah, I got one, *No douche-canoes allowed*," Jenna grumbled.

"Too obvious," I objected, shaking my head. I glanced over at the TV where Mal Reynolds was facing off against the alliance commander. "We should make an all-girls club. No boys allowed. Just like grade school."

"We can make Heath an honorary member!" Alex chimed. Heath had met the girls a few weeks back, and they'd all gotten along well.

"Our password should strike fear in the hearts of men everywhere," Jenna said with a gleam in her eye.

"I've got it!" Alex said. "Our password is: *I aim to misbehave.* And where those boys are concerned, that is *definitely* the truth!"

"Even though Orin so wants to go out with you, Alex," Jenna said with a smirk. "He'd totally drop this ongoing vendetta if you did."

"Hell to the no!" she hissed.

Jenna approached us, holding out her hands. "So say we all? Our club—we won't even name it. We'll call it the Club That Shall Not Be Named. Girl power!"

I put my hand on top of Jenna's, and Alex rested hers atop mine. "We aim to misbehave!"

"Maybe we can allow cute guys to be temporary members? Must be *extremely hot*, though." Alex chewed her lip, thinking.

"We can make Jack Eversea our mascot!" Jenna giggled. "He's so dreamy." Jack was Jenna's celebrity crush du jour.

"Okay, exceptions for hot guys. Especially dark-haired guys." Alex nodded.

"I like blonds and redheads better," I chimed while weirdly wondering what color hair FallenOne had, then promptly reminded myself that I wasn't going to think about him like that anymore.

Both girls frowned at me. I always had to be the voice of dissent, didn't I? Figured...

Soon after, we began our nefarious plans to escalate this cycle of pranks against the boys in the building.

Hey, I lived seven miles away from this building so I was safe from their retaliation. Therefore, I happily participated and hanging out with the girls was fun. It was *real.*

At this point in my life, *real* was just what I needed.

Chapter 10:
SWF seeks MHM

"**Y**ES. JUST LIKE THAT! OHHHH BABY!"

The neighbors across the way were at it. *Again.*

Due to the hot weather, I had my window open, which meant it was perfectly positioned, despite the distance, to pick up the fact that he was in the perfect position to "pound her like a hammer."

They had sex all the time. All. The. Damn. Time. You'd think it was the best thing ever to do. Or that it might be going out of style tomorrow.

Shit. They needed a hobby or something.

"Yes. God, yes! Yes! Oh Jesus." As far as I could tell, they didn't even go to church on Sundays, though their numerous exclamations seemed to profess deep belief in a higher power.

Jeez, studies or not, I needed to get the hell out of this apartment and away from the all-night sex-a-thon for a few hours.

I texted Heath and asked him if he wanted to grab dinner. As long as we picked some place cheap and air-conditioned, I'd be happy as a clam.

He picked me up a half hour later, just as the smell of cigarette smoke began drifting up from the neighbors' window. They'd be at it again later tonight, for sure.

We sat at the sandwich shop down the street—no chance to chill in the air-conditioning, but at least we were able to park our sticky bodies in front of a giant, high-powered fan.

I poked at my greasy—and overly salty—potato chip crumbs.

"You okay?" Heath asked.

"Mm," I mumbled distractedly.

Heath bit into his extra-large Italian sub on onion roll and watched me with wary eyes. He waited, well aware that I'd come out with it sooner or later. He didn't have to wait long.

I dropped the last bit of food onto my plate. "What's the big deal about sex, anyway?" I was only aware that I'd asked that in a slightly too-loud voice when heads at the next table turned in my direction. I let out a frustrated sigh, my face burning.

Clearing my throat, I swallowed and ignored their stares until they went back to their previous conversation. Heath gazed at me with his mouth hanging open.

I made a face at him. "Catching flies?"

He rolled his eyes. "I can't believe you just asked me that. Have your neighbors been knocking boots again?"

I blew out a breath. "It's the only thing they *ever* do. They need a TV or something."

Heath's grin grew sly. "Nothing on TV is half as fun as what they are doing."

"But do they have to let the whole damn world know? I mean, this woman is…loudly emotive…about her orgasms."

Again, the sound of my voice must have risen because those heads turned once more. My eyes narrowed as I stared back at them. "Oh, just go back to your food and your own conversation!" I barked and their eyes widened. Heath was red-faced and barely breathing from cracking up so hard.

After the group resumed talking to one another—probably about me. I turned to Heath, holding up both hands, each pointing the middle finger straight up on either side of my face while I stuck my tongue out at him. It only made him laugh harder. And after a few minutes of watching him fight to breathe, I had to admit that it was infectious. I started to laugh too, damn it.

This situation truly was ridiculous. He cleared his throat and wiped his eyes. "You either need to channel Meg Ryan and give your horny neighbors a scene like the one from *When Harry Met Sally,* or download some good loud porn and blast it back at them next time."

I rolled my eyes. "I'm sure they'd only find that a turn-on."

He shrugged, wiping tears from his eyes. "Probably so."

I blew out a frustrated breath. "I don't get it."

"Oh, my dear, some day you will. If you ever bother to date, that is."

"I'm perfectly aware that orgasms are enjoyable."

"Orgasms from sex with another person are even better," he quipped.

I busied myself with brushing up the stray crumbs at my place setting. "I don't have to date someone to have sex with them." At least this time, I remembered to keep my voice low.

Heath blinked, bit into his sandwich and chewed thoughtfully. "True. But you don't go *out* to meet people, even just to hook up. And since you are painfully socially awkward—"

I scowled. "Jeez, Heath. You sure know how to boost a girl's confidence. I'm awkward and socially impaired. But I'm not ugly."

His brows rose. "You are *definitely* not ugly. Quite the opposite. Men check you out all the time when we're out together. *But* you're totally clueless about that fact—which is both endearing and a little pathetic."

Making a face to cover for the awkward moment, I didn't bother to correct his assumptions of my cluelessness. Ignoring the stares, come-ons and advances was a *choice.*

"Not when you make that face, though."

Picking up my crust of bread, I tossed it at him. It bounced off his massive shoulder and landed on the table. He scooped it up and threw it back on my paper plate.

"I'm just saying that if you want the opportunity to…explore…you need to make yourself available."

I laced my fingers together and sat up straight, mimicking an overly attentive student, blinking my wide eyes innocently. "Like should I run a personal ad on Craigslist? SWF seeks MHM for hot sex and virginal deflowering?"

Heath's forehead buckled. "MHM?"

"Majorly hot male."

He snorted. "Don't do Craigslist. You take your life in your hands with the crazies. I forbid it."

I bit my lip. "One of those swipe left or right apps, then?"

Heath's mouth twisted thoughtfully. "Make some friends. Go to a few parties. Stop spending *every* night gaming with me, Fallen and Kat. Or the immature goobers that Jenna and Alex always flirt with. *They* won't get you anywhere, either."

A group of rowdy high school students made their way past our table, bumping Heath's back. He threw them a glare and they all backed off immediately, hands upraised in surrender.

"Oh, you want me to stop gaming with you?"

He turned back to me with an exaggerated eye roll. "No, I didn't say *that*. I said stop gaming with us on your only spare night. Get out and enjoy your college years—especially now that they are almost over. You've only got a year left."

I shook my head vehemently while gripping my hands together even tighter. "I don't want to do the social thing. I don't want to spend time with a guy who will boss me around. Or worse—someone who will want to change me to fit his image of what he wants me to be."

I didn't look Heath in the eye as I said this to him. In many ways, I was describing *his* boyfriend. If I could help it, he'd never know how much I disliked Brian.

Theirs was definitely a relationship I wasn't interested in emulating. I didn't want *any* romantic relationships. I didn't see the need. I'd *never* had to rely on a man—from the moment I was born, even—and I never, *ever* would.

But sex...maybe sex could be good. I'd never know until I tried it, right?

It was just getting past that pesky virginity hurdle. No casual one-night stand dude would want a part in that. Would they?

"What about that Jon guy in your study group? He seemed nice when I met him."

I shrugged. Jon was a good-looking guy, but... he just didn't do it for me. There was something about him that put me off. Maybe just because he was so overly eager.

"He's definitely into you. That's no mystery," Heath said with a crooked smile as he threw down his last French fry. "You know, whoever it is, it doesn't have to be a big, long-term commitment. You're friends with the guy. Why not just do a friends-with-benefits thing or something?"

I rubbed my cheek, my gaze drifting as I considered it. It wasn't really a bad idea. Jon was nice enough. He was smart, attractive—if a little needy. I didn't want him hanging around forever as a boyfriend, but once I retook the MCAT, I wouldn't be in his study group. Nor would we share any of the same classes, since he was a year behind me.

I contemplated that possibility. He'd probably ask me out again. He'd been persistent in the past. But...could I go all the way with him? And would he back away afterward if I did?

I blew out a breath. "There has to be an easier way to do this."

Heath laughed. "Don't sweat it, Mia. If you stop being so...aloof and unavailable, it will probably take care of itself. Just don't do anything stupid, okay?"

I raised a brow at him. "Have you ever known me to do *anything* spontaneous and potentially self-destructive?"

His smile faded. "There's always a first time... so try to be your usual sensible self. I'm sure you'll get that cherry popped in no time. Just don't expect it to be the best experience of your life. And don't expect the first to be your forever-love or something. Also, don't give up on sex *because* that first time ends up being crappy."

I shook my head, grimacing. "Wow, when you put it that way, what the hell have I been waiting for? Hold me back before I find some big stud to deflower me!"

Fortunately, I'd remembered to keep my voice down. But just in case, I glanced over at the table next to us, relieved to see that it was now empty.

Heath took me home and we hung out for a little bit before he declared it "too damn hot." Not twenty minutes after he left, my neighbors started screwing again—loudly.

***

Mom was definitely hiding something. It had been nagging me since the day I'd seen that look in her eyes. When she'd implied that she should have hid her cancer from me to keep me from worrying.

Of course, I was hiding things from her as well.

My MCAT failure, for one thing. *And* the fact that I'd decided to play amateur sleuth the next time I went back to the ranch.

She caught me at her desk, rifling through her bills.

"What are you doing with my private papers?"

She'd just come around the corner to find me elbow deep in envelopes. Her face immediately flushed.

My eyes snapped to hers and we held each other's gaze for a long, awkward moment.

Mom was looking under the weather this weekend, and she hadn't seemed too happy about my surprise visit. Maybe she'd wanted to spend the weekend alone or in bed or something. As it was, she'd been sleeping in later than normal, and I'd taken advantage of that this morning to flip through her mail—bills, mostly, the regular kind, and a lot of medical bills to boot.

Under the faint flush, her face appeared sallow with that unnatural yellowing of a person who'd been through harrowing medical treatment. In addition, her cheeks were hollow. "I was, um, just tidying up," I croaked. Caught red-handed, my own face started to flush with heat.

"They don't need tidying up!" she snapped. "Why are you digging through my business?"

I slowly stood from the table and swallowed a lump in my throat.

"I, um, wasn't trying to be nosy." A bald-faced lie. My gaze drifted away from hers.

With her mouth pressed into a straight line, she bent and jerkily snatched up her mail then stuffed it into a giant manila envelope.

I folded my arms across my chest. "Mom. Are you in some kind of financial trouble?"

She heaved a sigh. "Mia, you need to stop being all up in everyone else's business and get a life of your own." She did an about-face, turned the corner and disappeared into her room.

I stood there, my jaw hanging open. Suddenly, there were tears in my eyes, sharp and prickly. My own mother thought I was a loser who didn't have a life.

It was like a punch to the gut.

I left the house and went out to the barn to spend some time whining to the horses. I had no idea what Mom was doing in the house. Obviously, she was feeling like crap this weekend, and a lot of her attitude had come from that.

But the rest of it?

Were those bills the source of stress she was trying to hide from me?

Why did people who loved one another try to hide so much from each other?

If Mom was in financial trouble, was the stress from it making her sicker? She definitely looked *worse* this weekend than she had before. And she'd finished chemo weeks ago…

Afterward, I ran to the store to buy her some of the foods she relied on when she was feeling sick. When I got back, her bedroom door was closed, the light off.

I could only assume she was napping.

I left her a long note with an apology and a lame excuse about how I had to get back to my studies.

Then I left, filled with more questions and a ton more worry than I'd had before I arrived.

Chapter 11:
She's Auctioning *What?*

I RETURNED EARLY ENOUGH ON SATURDAY AFTERNOON, affording me a rare chunk of time to blow off steam on DE alone. I was still stewing from Mom's snappy behavior, particularly her assertion that I didn't have a life.

And instead of trying to figure out how to go out and actually *get* a life, I licked my wounds at home on a Saturday night by gaming. By myself.

Luckily, I wasn't alone for long. FallenOne logged on about an hour after I did. I guess he had nothing better to do with his weekend, either.

Our two missing party members, however, had not hesitated to inform us previously that they were going to enjoy themselves. They actually had social lives—and sex lives to boot!

I wondered what had happened that Fallen was hanging out with me. He'd been hooking up with someone fairly regularly. Until recently, he casually mentioned going out with a "friend" or having "a date." And, as usual, he'd been mysterious about it. Only an occasional pronoun clued me in that it was a woman.

Or maybe because he was in the Eastern Time Zone, he'd already gone out and come back from his dates before gaming with us… Who knew?

*You tell FallenOne, *So why aren't you out on a date tonight, too, leaving me to grind my dailies alone?*

*FallenOne tells you, *Shrug. I dunno.*

Me: *Did things fall through with your "friend"?*

Him: *You're nosy. And why would you put friend in quotes?*

Me: *I guess it's just my way of abbreviating Friend With Benefits.*

Him: *Well, we used to work together. She recently moved on to something else. Haven't seen her much, and, honestly, we never hung out a lot...*

Me: *You just got together to hook up?*

Him: *Not *just to hook up, no...but...more often than not.*

Me: *Hmmm.*

Him: *What, hmmm? I take it you disapprove?*

Me: *Me? No...I'm just wondering how something like that comes about...a friends with benefits type of situation. Like there's someone you're hanging out with as a friend and you just decide to start sleeping together? Does it just happen or do you have a conversation about it ahead of time or...?*

Him: *You're overthinking it.*

Me: *I overthink *everything. I am the queen of overthinking.*

Him: *I can see that. What's got you so interested in all this?*

Me: *I dunno. I think it's time to ...move forward and experience new things—so to speak. But I have zero interest in relationships or dating. You seem to have a convenient set-up, so I was just trying to figure out how you did it.*

Him: *I'm sure you'll figure something out with a little of that brainpower.*

I could see that he was typing, but nothing was coming through. It was as if he were typing and deleting the lines—more than once. Finally, a message came through.

Him: *But you know, what's the rush, right? You've got tests and medical school and all that...*

Me: *The rush is that I don't want to be an octogenarian virgin, tyvm.*

Him: *Well, there's quite some time before you become an octogenarian.*

Me: *Oh, whatever. Let's just go kill stuff.*

Him: *Like you just killed that conversation? Okay, fine. How about we try out that new fireworks quest? Word on the street is that people are having a lot of fun with it.*

Me: *Blowing crap up is almost as good as killing stuff. I'm down for that.*

***

**Elosia has entered the world of Yondareth*

FallenOne and Eloisa are scrambling around the crater of a steaming volcano, dodging random pools of lava as they collect pockets of sulfur for their wicked concoction.

Hassim, the quest-giver, has provided them with a special collection container, along with a list of ingredients that they will need in order to help him with his magical—and explosive—creations. Once finished, they'll have to venture into the deepest, darkest caves of Yondareth to collect saltpeter...

"I hope this quest is worth it," Eloisa murmurs to FallenOne, holding her nose to block out the rotten egg smell of the sulfur. Even so, she manages to reach her scoop into a pocket of the yellow substance hiding under a rock and dump it into her clay container, corking it up tightly.

"Hassim makes beautiful fireworks," replies FallenOne, nodding. "I'm sure it will be a sight to see."

After arduous days of trekking across the land, the two adventurers end up in a dwarvish mining camp, where they trade their labor—repairing the minecart tracks—for lumps of raw copper. The metal is a vital ingredient to produce the fireworks' blue sparks, among the many other colors of the display.

It's a long and tireless quest, and finally, with all necessary ingredients gathered, they return to Hassim. The exotics chemist will assemble them into his famous creations in time for the Great Gnomish World Festival.

Both FallenOne and Eloisa are full of excitement and can't wait to participate.

"Aside from getting our own personal fireworks to set off whenever we want, I can't wait to help assemble the display for the Festival." FallenOne combs his hand through his snowy beard thoughtfully, a dreamy look in his eyes—it's as if he's picturing what it will be like.

Eloisa, however, has been silent ever since turning the ingredients over to Hassim. While the two adventurers wait for him to assemble his fiery rockets, they've been asked to create a clearing, build a platform and, once the rockets are ready, set them up properly. She's beginning to think that this is a lot of work for very little gain.

As the tasks have mounted, Eloisa has become less and less amused

"This is a great deal of trouble for nothing, I think," she pouts.

FallenOne straightens from his backbreaking labor, having assembled the platform and stands for the rockets. "We're almost done. You'll see! Once the sun goes down, there will be such a sight to be seen, and we'll be the great heroes who brought the special magic of Hassim's creations to all the inhabitants in these parts."

But there are still more tasks to be completed. Hassim is very specific about the layout of the rockets, which must be arranged in a particular pattern, as does the black powder that acts as a fuse.

Eloisa's cheeks grow red with frustration and even a little anger. She's at the end of a too-short tether of patience. And she's not going to suffer fools gladly.

She's going to fight back.

She grabs the majority of the rockets and the barrel of black powder before FallenOne even realizes what she is doing. Hauling them to the platform, she piles the explosives in a high mound.

"That's not how Hassim told us to do it!" Fallen protests when he finally catches up with her, still a little stunned that she can move so fast.

"I don't care," retorts Eloisa. "That's what he's going to get!"

Then she uncorks her keg of black powder and begins to spread it across the ground in intricate patterns and shapes. She also spells out words in a mysterious foreign tongue that FallenOne has never seen before.

He watches, eyes growing wider at the pictures her patterns seem to form. "That's not—you can't be—what—?"

"Watch me," Eloisa bites out as she throws down her empty barrel of powder and pulls out her flint and steel. "I'd advise you to stand back."

Eyes wide and jaw practically hitting the ground, FallenOne complies, backing as far away as he possibly can while still in a position to witness what is about to happen in this tiny hapless hamlet at the edge of the woods.

When she's ready, Eloisa ignites a spark at the end of a long and twisting trail of scattered black powder, which leads directly to the gigantic mound of fireworks, sure to explode once the fire reaches them.

"That's the last time I do their monkey labor all for a damn reusable firework that will sit in my backpack and take up room until I decide to destroy it!"

FallenOne can only shake his head as the fire follows the trail of black powder, meandering around the intricate shapes and foreign alphabet letters, wending closer and closer toward the heap of explosives at the center of the platform.

"I'm going to give them a show they'll never forget!" Eloisa shouts gleefully.

***

I watched the display on the monitor, a fist pressed to my mouth as I suppressed a cackle. I could sense Fallen's annoyance from here.

The powder ignited from where I'd set fire to it, and flames erupted, lighting up the patterns. I had no idea what was going through Fallen's mind as he witnessed my rebellion, but it sure was funny as hell to me.

Flames wound around two giant circles, stretching into an elongated shaft of light. A flare of white stars streamed from the very tip. Lights flickered in patterns and spelled out words.

"Fuck off, Hassim" was one. *"You suck, Draco,"* another. And other fun little messages.

FallenOne remained noticeably quiet until the trail of flames led to the grand finale—a giant-ass mound of fireworks heaped into a pile that all exploded at once, nearly burning my retinas with the on-screen obnoxious display of light.

The entire village—had it existed outside the realm of pixels and bytes—would have been demolished.

I giggled like a child as I witnessed my devastation—the giant smoking crater in the clearing, all tinged with black. In just a quarter of an hour, it would all go back to looking as it did before, for the benefit of the NPC villagers and the players who would venture there with their own quests to complete.

But I'd likely burned my own bridges—in a manner of speaking.

That thought just made me laugh harder.

*FallenOne tells you, *Cock and balls, Mia, REALLY?*

*Eloisa tells FallenOne, *It's funny! Hassim's quest *really was annoying af. Don't you think?*

Him: *It wasn't *that annoying.*

Me: *It was damn annoying. This game is full of annoying busywork quests like that. I'd had enough.*

Him: *Oh come on, it was an interesting quest. And a great reward! Not that YOU were around to receive it.*

Me: *Says you. I rebelled.*

Him: *So I noticed. You are quite the rebel.*

Me: *I like mixing it up, what can I say?*

Him: *I assume there will be a full and thorough review of this quest chain on the blog sometime soon?*

Me: *Of course, I took screenies and everything.*

Him: *Wow. You're going nuclear.*

Me: *Meh. If I was going scorched earth, you'd know it. This is nothing. They'll get over it. Maybe they won't make so many busywork quests in the future. Win-win for all of us players.*

Him: *Are you actually trying to school the creators of the game with your snarkfest of a blog?*

Me: *I simply offer another perspective.*

Him: *Yeah, ya do.*

I thought I'd get more of a laugh from FallenOne—or at least a mediocre "ha ha." Maybe my humor was too immature for him or something.

Or maybe, just maybe, I needed to go out and get a life. I chewed on my lip and tried to squelch that prick of despair that threatened to blossom into something more serious. Even depression, maybe.

Sometimes a girl needed an escape from her worries and fears. Something safe rather than destructive.

And that was exactly what the game was providing.

Once we made it back to town, we gathered our items to turn them in to the quest giver for another quest. This time it was a ruffian named Dirty Deena, who had raided an armory and was prepared to give us—surprise!—shiny new breastplates in exchange for the random items she needed.

We handed over our hard-earned seashells, mollusk-encrusted doubloons and torn sails salvaged from a sunken ship. Dirty Deena laughed and sang and danced a pirate jig. FallenOne, as a spearman, received a polished, studded leather breastplate that gleamed in the sunshine. I quickly emoted my excitement to him, cheering and clapping and roundly encouraging him as he popped on that badboy. He looked GREAT.

Me: *Show me the stats on the breastplate! I want to see how good it is.*

Him: *Yours will have the exact same stats!*

So I checked my own reward. A *noticeable* improvement to the breastplate I'd been wearing for the last three levels. But what did the graphic look like?

I removed my old breastplate from the "chest" slot in my character screen and equipped it. Then, I switched back to the main screen so I could see what the graphic looked like on my character avatar.

Cue sad trombones. *Wah wah waaaaaah.*

It was nothing more than a glittery bikini top, perfectly tailored to show off Eloisa's ample bosom and cleavage.

Cue female player RAGE.

Me: *W.T. Actual. F.*

Him: *It, uh, looks good on you.*

Me: *Shut it, spearboy. Before I take that spear and shove it where the sun don't shine.*

Him: *Touchy, touchy.*

Me: *You would be too if all of Yondareth were conspiring to force you to go into battle wearing nothing but an armored loin cloth. You wouldn't dig that, now would you?*

Him: *Well, no. But look on the bright side?*

Me: *Bright side? There's a bright side?*

Him: *Yeah, our breastplates have the exact same stats. Same armor class, same hit points. Same protection all the way around, but yours weighs a lot less.*

Me: *That's because it's TWO MICROSCOPIC TRIANGLES OF ALUMINUM FOIL.*

Him: *But there *is a plus side...*

Me: *Yup, you've convinced me. I'm now all for showing the whole of Yondareth my virtual cleavage. NOT.*

Him: *This isn't going to make you rage quit, is it?*

Me: *I've got my finger on the rage quit button even as I type!*

Him: *Deep breaths, Mia. DON'T do it. You know you love Dragon Epoch.*

Me: *I'd love it more if they remembered that not every woman wants to show their girls to the world.*

Him: *Maybe they are implementing changes even as we speak. Maybe they'll give women a choice of the type of armor they want to wear...*

Me: *I can't possibly be the only female who rails against this. I know Kat isn't a fan either.*

Him: *They'll take all our feedback to heart.*

Me: *You go ahead and keep hoping for that. Girls just want to look badass, ya know? More Joan of Arc and less Princess Leia in the gold slave bikini.*

Him: *But Leia killed Jabba while she was wearing that gold bikini. She was badass AND sexy as hell.*

Me: *Sigh. Maybe that was a bad example.*

Him: *Changes may very well be coming.*

Me: *OR more likely.... the next quest will give out skintight metal hotpants that match this bikini top!*

Him: */sigh*

Fallen continued to listen to me rant at length. First in chat, then when I'd gotten tired of typing, I turned on my headset and did it over the voice channel. Once I'd calmed down, we headed toward the town square, were we needed to do some housekeeping tasks to prepare for our next big quest binge with the group. There, we'd be selling our junk to vendors, buying food items and supplies, then putting extra stuff in the bank so we wouldn't have to keep carrying it around.

On my way to the bank in Cormir City, however, I came across a curious gathering. A female avatar—a sexy elf with miles of flowing golden hair down to her ankles and clad in the skimpiest of shiny armor, jeweled breast cups and all—stood on a platform surrounded by quite a few other characters.

The dialogue being shouted out in the general chat channel made it sound like there was a live auction going on. And from the looks of the set-up, it appeared as if the subject of the auction was the elf avatar herself.

FallenOne appeared just as perplexed as I was when I sent him a message asking him what in Yondareth was going on.

Him: *I have no idea. It appears that people are bidding on "alone time" with the elf, named LadyHaHa.*
Me: *Alone time? For what?*
Him: *Uhhh...*

I continued to follow the proceedings for a few minutes as Fallen emoted shaking his head and feigning disbelief. Eventually, the innocent little virgin girl—that would be me—caught on.

The elf girl was auctioning off cyber time. As in cybersex. People were offering to pay to have virtual sex chat with this "hot" elf woman, whose double G breasts weren't even real. Hell, she probably wasn't even played by a real-life female.

Me: *Holy crap. I can't even.*
Him: *Yeah. And here I thought I'd seen everything in my years of gaming... I'm speechless.*
Me: *You're always speechless. You only type in chat.*
Him: *Funny.*

We bantered back and forth like that for a little while longer, but Fallen soon let me know that he had to log off. Me, I stayed to watch the shitshow for as long as it lasted. Eventually, a winner was declared, the agreed-upon fee was exchanged and the two participants filed off into a private room somewhere in the basement of an inn to emote sexually to each other.

Wow. The oldest profession existed even in Yondareth. Disturbing or ingenious? I guess it depended... on so many things. Consent and age of accountability being first and foremost.

With a shrug and a frown, I made a note to investigate this phenomenon further when I had some extra time—possibly as a future subject for the blog. There were so many things at play here, and it could become a rather complex issue—most especially for the people who ran the game.

Over the next few days, I had to admit that elf girl gave me a lot of food for thought. If she was of age and the other participant was of age and she needed the gold...then why not?

Was anyone being hurt, really?

***

Our gaming group stopped playing over the holidays. Christmas break led me back to the ranch, where the Internet was less than stellar for gaming anyway. Heath was going to spend time with Brian's family in Northern California, and Kat had double shifts at work. Fallen had whatever the hell Fallen had, which he was not forthcoming about—no surprise there.

When I arrived home, not a word was spoken about our little spat. I was received with open arms, a hug and a kiss. And, thank all the powers that be, a more vigorous looking, if noticeably thinner, parent.

But... I was not dissuaded from getting to the bottom of her financial mystery. Only this time, I waited until she left the house on some errands before I began to snoop.

Her desk was completely clean. Suspiciously so.

It *never ever* looked that decluttered unless she'd purposely cleaned it to keep the contents out of my reach.

Undeterred, I went straight to her books. As I used to help her keep the books when I was a teen, I knew exactly what to look for.

I opened to the page that listed her outstanding bills and my jaw dropped. How could she be so far behind?

My mind raced as my eyes slid down the balance column. Mom still wasn't well enough to re-open the inn, and even if she were, the busy season didn't start until mid-spring.

Her bank balance was in the negative.

I went in search of her bill remittance notices. After about five minutes, I found them in the bottom drawer of her nightstand. I removed a fistful of late mortgage notices and a crapload of medical bills that I could hardly fathom.

Unpaid statements for her chemo treatment…charges for her prescription medications …bills for in-patient therapies. She'd had no medical insurance to cover any of them.

My hands shaking and my stomach in my shoes, I knew what I had to do.

Unlike Mom, I *did* have some money stashed away. It was only a few thousand that I'd been skimming off my scholarship and grant money by living frugally, in hopes of slowly building a nest egg to start medical school.

It was that money that I deposited into her bank that very day. When it cleared a week later, I pulled out her bills and balance book—while she was out watering and feeding the horses, of course—and mailed off the paid bills before she could protest.

That way, when I told her, it would be a done deal and she wouldn't be able to undo what I'd done.

I was able to cover almost all of the remittance forms outstanding.

Except for the mortgage. I had no idea how far behind she was, and I could only do so much with my little nest egg. I'd have to figure out the rest later.

What this meant for medical school, however, remained to be seen. *If* I even managed to pass the MCAT.

But I'd find a way.

Minutes before kissing her goodbye, I told my mom what I did.

"Mom, um, check the balance book before you pay anything, okay? And please don't be mad."

She looked at me as if I'd just spoken Russian before understanding slowly dawned.

"Mia…what did you do?"

I smiled. "You can't undo it. So being mad at me is not going to solve anything."

She paled. "Mia…"

"Goodbye, Mom. Happy New Year." I got into my car and shut the door.

"Stubborn goddamn girl," she muttered.

I rolled down the window. "Totally heard that. If I'm stubborn, it's because I inherited it from you."

She watched me pull away with worry and guilt in her eyes. I had no idea if that guilt was borne from the secret she'd been keeping or the fact that she'd needed her daughter to bail her out. Anyway, it didn't matter.

I tried as hard as I could to ignore that look of guilt. Maybe she still knew something that I didn't. Maybe there was more she was hiding.

Maybe, just maybe, this dark weight I'd been carrying inside me for the past few months—for the past *year*, really—was about to get heavier instead of lighter…

Chapter 12:
Manifesto, Ahoy!

"*ERP, OR EROTIC ROLE PLAY –SHOULD IT STAY OR SHOULD It Go?" –posted on the blog of* Girl Geek.

If it stays, there will be trouble…

Oh never mind, this blog post won't be quoting moldy old songs from the 80s today.

Instead, I'd like to talk about the darndest thing I encountered in Town Square on Dragon Epoch. A—ahem—professional erotic role-player.

Yes, you read that right. A professional who engages in erotic role-play.

That's right—she'll please your avatar for the right amount of virtual gold. She'll type dirty things to you in chat if you pay her for her time.

The oldest profession has found a place in Dragon Epoch. Is this type of behavior against the game's Terms of Service? You know, that screed that scrolls across your screen and you click "I accept" every time there's a change to it—but you never actually read it? We all know you just lie and say you did.

Well, I took one for the team and actually read it, so you don't have to. Draco's Terms of Service do not explicitly forbid naughty role-play, but they do, of course, dictate the appropriate use of game resources, particularly when minors are present. Because there are a lot of peeps under 18 playing this game—and boy, are most of them a pain in the ass—the age of the person behind the avatar is definitely something to keep in consideration.

Personally, I think that as long as the participants are consenting adults and they take pains to verify that fact to each other—both the ages and the status of consent—who am I to oppose what goes on in private chat?

Prostitution is illegal in many countries. Should its equivalent be made illegal in Yondareth? I think there's a healthy discussion begging to be had for either side of this argument. Chime in and share your opinion in the comments.

***

Brian and Heath broke up. Just like that. No warning.

Well, besides the fact that they had a crappy relationship, there was no big fight or eruption that caused it to happen.

One weekend Heath drove up to Anza with me to help my mom with some maintenance issues at the ranch, and when he got back, his condo was cleaned out. That little turd Brian didn't even leave a note. Just took his shit—and then some—and left like the cowardly child he was.

And Heath was devastated.

Cue Mia with her broom and dustpan to swoop in and clean up the shattered pieces. I always did suck at housework.

I told him to pack his laptop, some clothes and bring his sleeping bag over to my place so we could camp out. I couldn't keep a good eye on him where he was. When he hesitated, I insisted. Actually, I drove over there and packed his bag myself.

With slumped shoulders, he resigned himself to his fate. He was going to stay under my watchful eye until I was satisfied that he'd be okay.

We spent a lot of that week gaming, in between my classes, shifts at the job and studying for finals. Only a few more weeks, and I'd be on my last semester of school with no classes. I still had to face that unanswered question of what to do about medical school, though.

Babysitting Heath's broken heart served as an excellent distraction from my own problems.

"Guess what I read on the Dragon Epoch forums this morning?" he asked toward the end of that week.

"Were you trolling forums instead of getting your work done?"

He gave me a sheepish grin. "They're my most understanding and patient client. They'll wait. A little while, at least."

I took a deep breath and raised my brows but didn't reply. He seemed to be in much better spirits today, and I didn't want to say anything to ruin it.

"So you didn't guess…and you probably won't, so I'm just going to tell you."

I nodded. "Please do."

"There was a mysterious post on the forums this morning providing inside info that a 'secret quest' is being implemented in the game."

I stared at him, uncomprehending. "A *secret* quest? What do you mean?"

"Well, no one really knows. Just that we're supposed to be talking to all the NPCs, and there's going to be a storyline involving the Princess Alloreah'ala—or however you pronounce it. Some kind of mystery to solve that will involve finding clues."

Something about this new intel struck a chord. I frowned, remembering a conversation I'd had with my gaming group months ago...

I'd love it if there was a secret quest...Like something hidden in the game underneath the obvious quests. Maybe we'd have to look for clues or speak to NPCs in order to get a hint that leads us on secret quest chains.

What Heath just described to me sounded exactly like what I'd been talking about!

How weird.

They'd taken a suggestion of mind after all...

Or maybe *he* had suggested it?

Or maybe he *did* work there after all. Or knew someone who did—the same person who gave him all the inside info, like that secret, impossible-to-find place he took me to.

When I really thought about it, I was just happy to see my idea become a reality—or at least a *virtual* reality. It didn't really matter how it got there.

The possibilities were exciting! I couldn't wait to see what the game had done with the idea, if in fact it was more than just a rumor.

I scoured the boards after that, looking for any information I could find about the quest, listening for any rumblings that it was more than just a rumor. It could be virtual reality, or it could be just a publicity stunt. I wasn't going to blog about it until I knew for sure.

Unfortunately, FallenOne was scarcely online over the next few weeks, so pumping him for info was not an option. But he couldn't stay away forever!

***

Due to my now near-empty bank account and lack of financial cushion, I requested—and was duly granted—more hours at the hospital. *Good.*

Though sometimes the grunt work annoyed me, the fatter paychecks would help offset what I'd paid out for Mom's bills. Unlike my undergraduate program, I'd likely be unable to finance medical school with academic scholarships.

And there was still the question of Mom's mortgage...all those late notices troubled me. I had no idea how long they would continue, or how Mom would be able to scrape up the money to cover what she owed.

Therefore, the increase in hours was a good thing. It also meant more responsibilities at the hospital, as well as a good taste of what working in the medical field would actually be like.

It was interesting and tedious, long and exhilarating. I promised myself that I'd remember these experiences for when—if I actually made it that far—I become a doctor. Though a nurse's assistant's tasks were necessary and vital to the workings of a hospital, they were thoroughly exhausting. And frustrating. As a doctor, I'd try my hardest to have empathy and gratitude for those who worked in often thankless jobs.

"I'm here to get my bloodwork done, like the doctor requested," said an elderly female patient who was sitting at my station when I arrived for a shift one morning.

"Okay, ma'am," I replied. "Can you tell me which doctor requested it?"

She looked at me like I'd just jabbed her in the ribs, her eyes widening. "Oh, I don't know deary. He was tall. And thin."

A tall, thin man. I wasn't familiar with most of the doctors who worked in this department, but that description fit about half of the ones I did know.

"Er, and what type of bloodwork?"

She stared at me blankly. I waited. And waited. When no answer to my question was forthcoming, I readjusted my tablet against my hip. "What is your name, ma'am?"

"Johnson," she replied. "Elizabeth Johnson."

Oh well, shit. Could she have a more common name?

I typed her name into the system. Four Elizabeth Johnsons appeared. However, I still had the means to discern which one I wanted.

"What's your date of birth, ma'am?"

"That's kind of a rude question to ask, isn't it?" Her aged forehead crinkled. "Of a lady *my* age."

It was all I could do to keep from rolling my eyes. "Uh. I need to be able to find you in the system."

She glared at me suspiciously. "Hmm. Well. I was born on June 13th."

"Year?"

Her brows went up. "Isn't that enough to go on?"

I glanced down at the four Elizabeth Johnsons. Not one of them had the birthday June 13th.

"Uhh. Are you sure you're in the right place?"

Underneath her thick makeup, she flushed beet red. "Well, of course! I'm not *senile*."

I blinked. "I'm sorry, ma'am. I didn't mean to imply that. But...you're not showing up in my system under Elizabeth Johnson, and in order to find you by your birthdate, I need the year, too."

This went on for ten minutes before I finally convinced her to give me her "real" birth year, not the one—five years later—that she gave out in her social circle. Come to find out, she was listed under her second husband's last name.

Oh *brother*.

Once I located the right account, I saw that she had seven different doctors—and no order for blood labs. I knew this because I had to call each and every one of their offices to ask.

Oh God, spare me from the madness!

Returning home one night after a particularly trying time in the ER with a drunken man who vomited everywhere in between calling me every name in the book, I took the hottest shower imaginable. Of course, at my house, that only lasted all of three minutes because of my hot water situation. But in that brief time, I sobbed harder than I had in years. I just had to let it out.

Then I logged on.

And though I was primarily there to blow off steam, I had to admit I was a little dismayed that no one from my friends list was online. I checked. FallenOne hadn't been on in over a week! My heart sank a little...

I'd really been looking forward to chatting with him, but there had been no text messages, either. I picked up my cell phone and then thought better of it when I realized what time it was on the East Coast.

I made a mental note to text him in the morning and see how he was doing...

Turns out, I didn't have to. Twenty-five minutes later, Fallen's private message magically flashed on my screen. I tried not to examine too closely that little thrill that ran through me when I saw that it was him.

*FallenOne tells you, *Hey. How's the job going? They are working you a lot more than usual.*
*You tell FallenOne: *Meh. I'm tired all the time.*
Him: *What's with the increase in hours?*
Me: *Just money hungry, I guess...*

I'd decided not to get too specific about our money troubles—with anyone. I hadn't even spilled the beans to Heath, yet. Maybe I would eventually. But I had to figure things out first. Ultimately, the answer to my financial problems wasn't going to be this job. I'd crunched the numbers, and though I'd be able to live on my paychecks and the blog revenue, there wasn't going to be much of anything to replenish my savings.

Tears started welling in my eyes, and I ordered myself to stop that nonsense. I'd only allowed myself that brief collapse of emotion in the shower.

Me: *Feeling a bit down tonight.*
Him: *I'm sorry. Can I do anything to cheer you up?*
Me: *I dunno...can you? Got any dirt on that secret quest everyone's talking about?*

Him: *I'm afraid not. But how about mass pixel murder?*

Me: *Tempting...but no...*

Him: *I'm sorry. Want to talk it out?*

Me: *I'm not sure I even have the energy for that. You ever have those times in your life where things just don't go the way you expected?*

Him: *Is this about the test again? Are you torturing yourself about that?*

Me: *It's not just about the test.*

Him: *You should just take it again, you know. Take it and take it and take it again. Failure is just a way of learning. And with each attempt at the test, you learn more and you'll do better.*

Me: *I'm feeling like too much of a failure to even consider it. But really, it's more than just that damn test. It's only a fraction of my worries...*

Him: *I'm here for you. I'm your friend. Please let me know if there's anything I can do to help.*

Me: *I will. I promise. I know I just logged on, but I'm actually really exhausted. I think I'm just going to crash.*

Him: *Okay. But check in with me tomorrow, please? I don't want to have to worry about you all day.*

Me: *Okay. I promise :)*

Him: *Sleep well.*

Me: *Bye.*

I was drifting off before my head hit the pillow, but my mind was racing even as slumber took me. Strangely, the last thing I thought of was that weird scene in DE where the female elf in her shiny lingerie armor stood on the platform in the town square, auctioning herself off to the highest bidder.

If only it was that easy in real life…

I woke up with the idea fully formed in my brain, ready to be realized. I ran to my computer, opened the word processing program and began to type furiously.

Oh, this was a wild idea. An insane idea. I could never carry this out. I *would* never carry this out. But it was so insane, and I couldn't *not* write it down. It was just spitballing…right?

Right. And so I typed as fast as my fingers would allow me.

I will shock most of you, I think, by stating that at the nearly unthinkable age of twenty-two, I still possess an intact hymen. No, I won't answer any questions about why this is. Yes, I am heterosexual. NO, I won't go out on a date with you…

And on I typed, not even knowing if or when I'd show this to another soul. But I couldn't stop. I couldn't stop.

Chapter 13:
WTF Did I Just Read?

To: Heath, Persephone (Katya), FallenOne

From: Mia

Re: A Wild Idea

So, on a whim, I wrote a "manifesto." I'm not even sure at this point what it means or what I'll do with it. But I'd be honored if you read it and tell me what you think.

Hugs,

Mia

Attachment: Virgin Manifesto.doc

***

I went to my study group.

Jon asked me out. *Again.*

I had to think of another lame excuse on the fly. *Again.*

This was getting tedious. I vowed to brainstorm with Alex and Jenna a list of excuses I could have handy in the future. He'd have to figure out eventually that I wasn't interested...*right?*

And as for him being "the one" to relieve me of my burden of virginity…I had already decided against it.

Not that I was on board with the idea of auctioning it off, either. I was waiting for feedback first.

When I returned to my studio, the phone was ringing as I stumbled up the stairs. It was the landline, because, as always, I was low on minutes—and low on money—so I'd asked people to call the landline instead.

I got to it just as whoever it was hung up without leaving a message.

Damn it.

I guessed it was probably Heath, so I waited until settling in before getting back to him.

First, I checked my email and discovered a reminder for the upcoming MCAT retake. Without hesitating longer than five seconds, I followed the link, logged into the site and pushed my test date back three more months. I'd done this two times before, since they allowed a window of thirty-one days or more before the test to move the date.

This was starting to become a sick little game of Avoid The Test Date, no less intense than a fifth-grade game of tag on the playground. With that same tight feeling in my chest lessening, I knew—just like I'd known those two times before—that I'd done the right thing.

Of course, I was almost certainly dooming myself to skipping a year before I could attend medical school. My fear had caused me to wait too long, and now I'd pushed myself out of the window of opportunity to apply for the upcoming year. I swallowed the lump in my throat and packed that heavy burden away with the rest of the worry, anxiety and guilt that had been weighing me down as of late.

Without another thought, I scrolled down my inbox list to check and see if there were replies to my manifesto. Indeed, there were emails from both Persephone and FallenOne waiting for me.

To: Mia
From: FallenOne
Re: A #%@$& idea

What the fuck did I just read???
No seriously. WTF is this?

Ooookay then. Fallen wasn't on board, apparently. Or he was taking it as a joke.

I *had* half-jokingly sent it, so… that was understandable. I replied quickly, hoping I'd get clarification from him later.

I scrolled down to Kat's response.

To: Mia
From: Katya Ellison
Re: A kickass idea

This was awesome. Are you going to do it? It's kinda scary but also super exciting, and…to be honest, I'm a little jealous I didn't try to cash in monetarily on getting my v-card punched! You're a smarty.

So… are ya going to do it?

That was more like it... So I had one yay and one nay—although possibly a joking one. And Heath, the wild card. It was time to find out what *he* thought.

I picked up the phone and called him.

"Yo, doll," he answered, sounding a lot better than he had in the three weeks since Brian left. Heath was starting to heal at last...though I made a point to check in with him every single day.

"Hi!" I squeaked. "How are we today?"

"Exhausted. I've been pushing through this project deadline. Just posted the last bit of work about an hour ago. Now I'm sitting in front of the TV mindlessly vegetating."

I paused. "Oh okay, so you didn't just try to call me?"

"No, why?"

"I was coming home from study group and didn't make it to the phone. No message."

There was rustling, like he was readjusting how he was sitting on his squeaky leather couch. "You know I always leave a message. Even though I hate doing it."

"True. So I take it you haven't checked your email?" I fiddled with my phone cord, suddenly feeling nervous without understanding exactly why.

"Nope. I haven't done *anything* but work on that website update. Why, did I miss something?"

"Uh, I sent something out to you, Kat and Fallen for an opinion. The other two got back to me, sorta, and I was just wondering what you thought."

"Sec. Opening up my laptop..." I cleared my throat, suddenly wanting to get off the phone while he read it. Did I *really* want to hear his real-time reaction? "I'm gonna—"

"This is a joke, right?" he cut me off. "A Virginity Manifesto?"

"I just wrote it on a lark."

"Okay." He paused, and I could only assume he was still reading. I fidgeted in my seat, self-conscious.

"Interesting treatise, Mia. What's it for? Are you defending your right to stay a virgin without judgment, or somehow trying to say you want to profit from being a virgin?"

I blinked. "I, uh, the latter, actually."

A long pause. "You lost me. Can you go back to the beginning?"

"A few weeks ago, Fallen and I were on the game together because you were... out, and so was Kat..." Best not remind him that he was out on a date with the now-ex BF. "We worked on that asshole fireworks quest, and I was feeling punchy. When we got back into the town, some lady was up on stage in the town square auctioning herself for cyber."

He laughed. "Yeah, I've seen her around before. She propositioned me one time. Had to let her off easy and tell her that she was barking up the wrong tree. I'm gonna assume she inspired you to blog about her auctioning off cybersex?"

"She did inspire me, but not just to blog about it."

He laughed. "Surely not put your*self* up for auction..."

I hesitated, hoping he'd come to the right conclusion, fearing the trepidation already apparent in his voice.

After an awkward minute or so, he broke the silence. "That's hilarious, Mia. I guess you got me. Scared the shit out of me there for a minute."

I swallowed. "I, uh... I wasn't joking around."

Silence.

More silence.

I couldn't even hear him breathing. Nothing.

"Of all the hare-brained shit I've ever heard of—and I've heard my fair share, considering who I was just in a relationship with—I've never heard something this ridiculous. *Please* tell me this is a joke."

I sighed, tempted to just laugh it off. I wasn't even committed to this idea, right? This was all…academic. I was trying it on for size—so I told myself. But something deep inside told me *not* to give in. "I just said it wasn't," I answered in a quiet voice.

Another long stretch of silence. I snatched up a pen and began doodling on the back of an envelope. Loops and squares, all interconnected. My pen traced the same lines over and over again, etching deep grooves into the paper.

"I know we just talked about getting your cherry popped, but this is *not* what I meant. You also asked me if you were ever known for doing anything stupid, and up until *now*, I agreed. Shit. This is madness. Why would you even consider doing something like this?"

I shifted in my seat. "I think I outlined it pretty clearly in the manifesto."

"Bullshit. This is about money. Tell me what's going on."

"Money is an added benefit, yes. I'd like to have a way to pay for medical school and, um, other things."

"What other things?"

I briefly explained to him about my mom's bills and the late mortgage notices. He sucked in a breath and stabbed back. "Why didn't you tell me? I could have helped you…"

"You were going through your own mess at the time," I replied, referring to the breakup. "And I had it under control, as much as I could."

"I don't get this at all. You've had a rough patch with failing the test and your mom getting sick, and now the financial issues. I get it. But that's all it is—a rough patch. And it will pass."

"Maybe I want to do something proactive instead of waiting around while life throws obstacles at me." My voice trembled as my conviction grew. "Maybe I want to overcome—"

"How would you even carry something like this out? In case you need a reminder, prostitution is illegal in this country."

I stared unseeingly at the blank patch of wall in front of me. "Not *everywhere* in this country. There are legal and safe brothels in Nevada. I could contact one of them and ask for help."

He let out what sounded like a growl of frustration. "I can't even with this bullshit, Mia."

My stomach knotted. Heath's approval meant so much to me that proceeding without it almost stopped me cold. *Almost...* "I'd love to have your support, but I could continue without it, if necessary."

"You want me to *help* you auction yourself off to some stranger? You do realize this is to have sex with someone, right?"

I rolled my eyes, not dignifying that stupidity with a reply. The circles and squares had transformed into angry x's now, scratched so deeply into the paper that they were marking the layer underneath as well.

"I can't force you to help me if you are unwilling …" My voice shook, but there was a new possibility arising. *Could I do this?*

Heath mumbled something incoherent—probably riddled with lots of bad words—and then said, "I'm exhausted and I can't think straight, and I'm really not processing all of this very well. I want to meet with you about it tomorrow."

"Okay. I'm here and available for that."

"Promise me you won't do *anything* or proceed in any way until we talk."

"If we are meeting tomorrow, there's not much I can do between now and then." I shrugged though I knew he couldn't see me.

"No contacting brothels or whatever. Just sit on this for twenty-four hours. Please, it's all I ask."

"All you ask before you work on changing my mind?"

His sigh was longsuffering. "Just promise me."

"Okay, I promise."

We hung up, and just as quickly I put my face in my hands, rubbing my eyeballs. Though I hadn't let on to Heath, indecision was still gripping me. I loved the *idea* of the auction but hated the reality of it. I loved the statement I'd be making while hating that I'd have to commit to at least one night of sex work to accomplish it.

This would probably all be academic. It would amount to nothing. I didn't have the guts to see this through.

Did I?

When in turmoil, I did what I liked to do best—dressed in shorts and running shoes and then, instead of making my way out the door, booted up the computer and logged into the game.

I didn't know why I was expecting Fallen to be on. He was rarely on during the day. But the past few times I had logged in—no matter what time of day or night—he logged on soon after. It was almost as if he'd figured out my pattern for logging in and knew when to look for me.

And I wouldn't admit to myself outright that I *was* logging on to find him. Or waiting for him to find me.

After about an hour of running around doing solo stuff, a notification lit up on the dialogue box of my screen. I was more than a little disappointed when I saw that it was Katya, not Fallen.

She immediately messaged me.

Persephone tells you, Hey babe! Turn on your voice chat!

I clicked on my settings menu, since it had been a while since I'd turned on voice chat. Lately, it tended to make my game lag, so I hadn't been using the feature as much as before.

"Tell me! Was that Virgin Manifesto for real?"

I fiddled with my headset, readjusting it so the speakers covered my ears. "Yeah…yeah," I said, trying to hide the doubt in my voice.

"Wow, you're a baller, girlfriend. I'm impressed."

"Thanks. Glad *someone* approves."

"Oh? Did Heath say something? Guys are so weird about stuff like that."

"Yeah." I sighed. "They aren't taking it well."

"*They*? Who else? *Fallen?*"

I squirmed in my seat, grabbing a Star Wars Happy Meal toy that I'd collected ages ago and fiddling with it. "Yeah, he sent a very terse reply. I answered, telling him it was for real, and he hasn't replied since."

"It's only been a few hours, right? I wouldn't sweat it. He's got a weird schedule, remember?"

I tossed my completely inked-over envelope into the trash. "Yeah. I guess."

"And besides, he's probably butthurt about it, since he's got a thing for you."

I frowned. "What on earth are you talking about?"

"Oh c'mon, don't play coy. I know you've probably suspected it, too. Remember our application of the scientific method?"

I scoffed. "We were messing around. He doesn't have a 'thing' for me!" I shifted again and tried to ignore that same feeling I got when I was looking for him and he showed up. There's no way a crush like that could go anywhere, so it was best to suppress it as soon as possible. "How could he? We've never seen each other in person... never even had a decent conversation on the phone."

"Love finds a way..." she said in a sing-songy voice.

Love... now that was just crazy talk.

I scoffed. "You're insane."

"*Lots* of people find love online. And tons of people connect via online games like DE. It's not impossible, Mia."

"But in order to be in love, it has to be reciprocal. And it's not."

"Are you *sure?* I've long suspected you might have a little crush, too."

I was blushing furiously, now thankful this wasn't video chat because of the heat radiating off my face and chest from embarrassment—and yeah, acknowledgement—of what she was saying.

"I think you're delusional and projecting," I snapped.

She heaved a long sigh. "If you say so. Let's go kill stuff…maybe you'll have everything figured out about your auction after you commit virtual slaughter."

"It is always good for loosening the creative mind." I laughed.

And so we did. Instead of doing quests, we parked ourselves in a populous corner of a dungeon and pulled respawns, killing them over and over again.

Fallen never logged on that night, and this brought about a disappointed, edgy feeling underneath everything else. Katya's suspicions both scared and thrilled me at the same time. But what did any of this mean, in the long run? And how could anything worthwhile arise between us when he constantly withheld everything from me? FallenOne could never be anything more to me than a good online friend. In a few years, we'd likely be strangers to one another.

Nevertheless, after all that killing and banter with Katya, I was still no closer to deciding what I was really going to do about the manifesto.

***

For the first time in a long time, I struggled with insomnia. And when I finally did drift off to sleep, I experienced dreams every minute, causing me to wake up exhausted. They popped up persistently, like respawns in the game, coming at me over and over again.

In one dream, I was at the ranch in Anza…only it was deserted. I was entirely alone. My mom, all the ranch hands, even the horses were gone. It was like I was the last person on earth. I wandered the place, calling out for her—for anyone— with no reply. The wind and my calls echoed back to me without an answer.

The next thing I knew, I was sitting at a desk in a brightly lit classroom, a blank test in front of me. But I couldn't read it or understand a thing. The paper was covered with meaningless symbols—or perhaps a foreign language that I couldn't recognize. I had a stack of pencils lined up perfectly on my desk, all with pristine, sharp points, ready to be used. But as each minute passed and I stared at that paper, it grew harder and harder to comprehend. This was my last chance at the MCAT and I was utterly lost.

I woke up gasping for air.

And with a new conviction. I hated this feeling of powerlessness. I was going to be proactive. It was time to take control.

Not by finally retaking that goddamn test, though. I wasn't quite ready for *that*.

Later in the afternoon, Heath appeared in my doorway, a laptop bag slung crosswise over his massive chest and a solemn cast to his handsome features. Without a word, I stepped aside and let him in.

He settled gingerly onto my creaky old couch, and I took the beanbag chair on the floor. Then I offered him a chilled water bottle, which he uncapped and promptly downed half.

"I really *really* need to know you aren't punking me with this BS," was how he began.

My eyebrows twitched upward and I chewed on my lip. "I'm not that cruel."

Heath reached over, unzipped his bag and pulled out his device, opening it with jerky, determined movements.

"I thought up a list of alternatives to the fuckwit auction."

My ire rose and I folded my arms across my chest. "I'm a fuckwit, now?"

"*You* aren't. The auction, however, is. Just hear me out." He gestured to the list. Whoa…he'd really thought things through, hadn't he? "First off, you are done with your coursework, so you can get a better paying job than the one you have at the hospital."

I frowned. "But the one at the hospital is not just for pay. It's to help me build my CV for medical school. I need the job for my résumé."

"Okay, then you can get a second job."

I nodded. "Fine. At a strip club, maybe? They pay well, I hear. I'm a shitty dancer, though."

"Then you could wait tables at Hooters."

I looked down at my less than ample chest. "Only a gay man would suggest that I had sufficient assets for a job at Hooters."

"Then a regular waitress job. Or a receptionist. Or just *anything* that doesn't involve you lying on your back and spreading your legs."

I stared at him with baleful eyes. "Next?"

"You could sell off your valuables."

I started to laugh so hard I couldn't breathe. My beater car could maybe get me a thousand or two—that was about it. And he knew damn well I had no valuables. No jewelry, no expensive electronics. Nada.

"Okay, okay. I was just hoping maybe you had an heirloom or something."

"Yes, I have the millions in T-bills from my deadbeat Biological Sperm Donor. But I was saving those for a special occasion."

Heath rolled his eyes and resumed reading from his laptop. "There are loans."

I held up my hands. "I owe thousands already. Please, stop. This isn't helping. You don't think I've gone through all of this already? How on earth could I earn enough in a short period of time to help with Mom's mortgage issue?"

He shook his head. "You don't even know how much she owes."

"It's thousands. Of that I'm certain. Now, please spare me the patronizing."

He flushed. "I wasn't trying to…" He closed his eyes and took a deep breath.

"I know you mean well," I began, and he gritted his teeth.

"*You* can stop with the patronizing, too. I'm just trying to talk sense into your head and show you that this drastic and destructive course is *not* the only option."

I hugged myself as if trying to summon strength from it, but I remained silent.

Heath shook his head, shifting his weight while the couch groaned. "I can't tell you how strongly I feel about this. It was all harmless discussion back when it was just about you losing your virginity. Now you want to *monetize* it? And for what reason? If your mother found out what you were doing in order to help her, she would *freak*."

I leaned forward, shooting fire from my eyes. "She's *not going* to find out, now is she?"

Heath grimaced. "Not from me. But Mia, this is madness. Truly, I have to say it's madness. Please just think about this and—"

I stomped my foot on the ground. "I *have* been thinking about it. *Constantly*. So don't mansplain to me."

He laughed and rolled his eyes, throwing his head back on the couch in exasperation. "I'm not mansplaining. Jeezus. I just… I want the best for you. I want you to have a better experience for your first time than what you're planning. I mean—some skeezy stranger somewhere in a hotel room or whatever?"

"Well, you said the first time isn't all that great anyway. Why not do it with a long list of rules and stipulations. It is *my* body, and *I* control what happens to it."

Heath went absolutely still and let out a long breath. He straightened his head, meeting my gaze. "So *that's* what this is about? Having control over the situation? Because of what Zach did to you in high school?"

I refolded my hands. "Control is very important to me. *Especially* after this year—almost losing Mom. Failing the MCAT. It's not just about what happened in high school. It's about everything."

Heath nodded, his mouth slightly agape. "But not just control over this one night. You want control over it all. *How* it happens. *When* it happens. What happens afterward…" His voice drifted off.

I held his gaze and nodded slowly. This all seemed perfectly obvious to me, but he was coming to some lightbulb-moment realization.

"I think I get it now...the control thing." His fixed stare continued.

I took a deep breath and let it go. "No need to psychoanalyze me. You aren't my shrink."

"Maybe you should have a chat with yours."

I shrugged. "Maybe I will...when I go up there next." I had no intention of doing it, mind you, but if it made Heath feel better to think that I might—why not add that to my argument? "Ultimately, it's my body. My decision. And I'll do it with or without your help, Heath."

"Riiiight..." He nodded. "*But* if you want my help, you have to convince me you are doing this for the right reasons."

I bit my lip. "And what are the *right* reasons, Heath? Whatever reasons I have for this should be the right reasons for me."

His features clouded. "I'm sorry. That sounded arrogant, didn't it? Like I was in some position to determine what's best for you. I just—I just don't want to see you get hurt, Mia."

I stood up and slid onto the couch beside him—what little room there was with his big body and laptop bag. "I know you didn't mean to sound arrogant. But yeah, you know I'm a big girl."

"Mia." He shook his head as he leaned forward. "You have to be sure. And you *have* to be careful. This is some heavy shit we're talking about here."

I laughed shakily. "I know. It scares the shit out of me, too." And it was true... my heart was thrumming in my carotid artery, making it hard to swallow. This moment—this blink of an eye where I solidified the resolve to do this—was absolutely terrifying.

And...*liberating.*

"There is so little I can do for her. So little within my power to help her. But *this* I can do. Heath...*please*..."

Heath's eyes closed and he pinched the bridge of his nose. "I'll help you, then. But only if you let me control it all."

And he thought I was having control issues? My eyebrows arched. "Only if that means you don't call the whole thing off."

He shook his head. "No. I won't do that. You'll ultimately call the shots on whether or not this thing goes through. But...I want a say on the details. How you set this up. How you protect yourself. The legalese. I have a lawyer friend who can help, I think."

I nodded. "I can do that. I can..." My voice faded out, suddenly choked with emotion. "Heath...thank you."

"Don't thank me yet. We have no idea how this whole shitshow is going to turn out." He leaned forward and pulled me into one of his massive bear hugs. "You know I'd do anything for you, and I'm going to do everything in my power to protect you."

"I know. Thank you. And I'm going to do everything in my power to not need that protection."

"Whatever skeeve out there who wins this auction and goes to bed with you—"

"Let's not think about it like that." I spoke into his shoulder. "Maybe there's a nice person out there who is interested in making sure my first time is a good one."

"And you think *I'm* an idealist."

"Well, whoever he is, *I'll* think of *him* as a way of making my future secure and proving my new paradigm." I tried to ignore the lump in my throat. "It'll be okay, Heath," I said and cut myself off abruptly when my voice shook. His hold on me tightened, but he said nothing. I closed my eyes and rested my head on his shoulder.

I just hoped whoever this guy was, he'd leave a nondescript and bland mark on my past—enough to not make a lasting impression. It would be one night of my life, and nothing else would change but the size of my bank account and my status as a virgin.

Simple as that.

***

"Okay, turn the other way and, um, lean up against the rocks." Heath held the camera out in front of him, peering at the viewfinder on the back while clicking away.

A week had passed since our conversation in my apartment. To his credit, Heath hadn't tried to change my mind again.

I complied with his instructions, trying to ignore the curious onlookers who glanced at us as they walked past. I was in a yellow and black polka-dot bikini, the beach wind whipping my hair every which way. I pushed it out of my face and tilted my hips to the right, feeling simultaneously silly and daring.

Ugh. I *never* wore bikinis. It wasn't about disliking how my body looked. I'd always felt fine in my own skin—aside from the less than ample chest, anyway.

But the *irony.* The sheer irony of posing in a real-life cloth bikini for the benefit of this auction when I'd spent so much of my time railing against the metallic bikinis so often clothing virtual female avatars…

It felt hypocritical, to be honest.

I was out of my depth. I'd already mentally accepted the fact that I would be going to bed with some stranger who had paid for the privilege of deflowering me. *That* I had accepted. But this final straw, posing sexily in this bikini, objectifying myself on the jetty of Corona Del Mar, seemed to be approaching the limit to this entire illicit scheme of mine.

My throat was tight the entire time, and strangely, I felt detached from my surroundings as Heath ordered me to pout for the camera. Were I not operating in this weird fugue state outside my own reality, I would have laughed at him.

Shit just got real.

Later that same day, Heath sent the pics over to me. They were decent—cropped so as to hide my identity.

I put the post together. First, I listed the *Virgin Manifesto* along with the photos and a link to the auction site. That link went to another server and site entirely located outside of the country, just as Heath had set up. I'd given myself three weeks to run the auction, and hopefully that would minimize any media frenzy that might crop up. With any luck, soon afterward, the deal would be carried out.

I scheduled the post for early the next morning while I was still at work, hoping I'd put enough safeguards in place to protect my anonymity.

Aaaaand I stayed away from social media that day. I went to work then study group and didn't even open my browser when I got home.

I avoided emails, too.

Instead, I logged on to DE and checked my friends list. No one was on. I ran a few minor quests, and sure enough, a half hour later, my notification screen lit up.

Your friend, FallenOne, has logged on.

My screen immediately flashed with a new private message from Fallen.

FallenOne tells you, You're actually going to let some stranger fuck you for cash?

My jaw dropped and I drew back from the screen. Wow. He wasn't going to mince words tonight, was he? He came out with gloves off. So very unlike him, actually. I clenched my jaw and put my hands back on the keyboard to type my response.

You tell FallenOne, That's a rather crude way of putting it. It's about my new paradigm. It's a feminist statement.

Him: *It's prostitution. You are willingly turning yourself into a common hooker.*

Me: *One time. And it will all be done in a perfectly legal way.*

Him: *Who gives a crap about the legalities? What you are doing is destructive. To YOURSELF. To your future.*

Me: *It's MY body.*

Him: *So says every drug addict, every alcoholic, every anorexic out there.*

Me: *Are you interested in having an adult conversation about this, or are you going to just insult me?*

Him: *If I thought you'd listen, I'd chat your fingers off all night.*

Me: *Okay. Well, I'm listening, then.*

Him: *Mia, have you considered how this will affect your future? What about if you meet someone you fall in love with... will you tell your future husband that you were a whore for a night?*

Me: *Will you tell your future wife about screwing that girl on the conference table at your uncle's office? What difference does it make? How much do people really know or want to know about their partners' previous lovers?*

Him: *That's not the same. At all.*

Me: *And if you fell in love with a woman and were about to marry her, would it make a difference to you if she'd told you she sold sex for money in the past? You'd break up with her because of it?*

We went back and forth like that—for hours. My fingers ached and still he typed. Sometimes big paragraph-long treatises about the destructive nature of sex work and how these actions really were counter to the feminist message that I'd conveyed on my blog—no matter how much I'd couched them in that "silly manifesto."

Fallen grew more and more frustrated and became more and more insulting as the night wore on. When my eyes were teary and gritty from yawning too much, I knew I had to get to bed soon. But I didn't want to be the first one to give up on this conversation.

And for Fallen, I could tell it was *very* important to him that I change my mind.

However, he refused to actually tell me why he felt so strongly. *Yes,* it was obvious he felt strongly about the subject, but apparently not very strongly about *me*. He still held back about himself. So clearly I wasn't important enough…

Him: *In the end, you are willingly making yourself damaged goods.*

Me: *Excuse me. But I don't see it that way at all. Don't get all judgey on me. You're like Malcolm Reynolds and his hypocritical disrespect for Inara.*

Him: *This isn't Firefly, Mia. This is real life, not TV.*

As I'd expected, he'd understood the reference perfectly.

Me: *It's an example.*

Him: *Besides, Mal respects Inara just fine. What he hates is her profession. And you are NO "registered companion" like Inara is. Which is something that doesn't even exist in our world. Firefly is a figment of Joss Whedon's imagination. You spreading your legs for some disgusting John is not.*

Me: *Stop talking to me like I'm a child.*

Him: *I'm just trying to talk sense into you.*

Me: *How I lose my virginity is my business only.*

Him: *And, of course, the business of the disgusting pervert who buys you.*

Me: *I'm not going to put up with that shit. Take it elsewhere.*

Him: *Well, don't let me keep you any longer. I'm sure you want to get on with your auction. May the best creeper win.*

*FallenOne has logged off from Dragon Epoch

I sat dumbfounded, staring at the screen, noting the weight that dropped in my stomach. My eyes started to sting.

Just a little...

Maybe... maybe I'd never see him online again.

And maybe this auction was a mistake. But it was mine to own.

Perhaps he was right and the ramifications of this one night would reverberate throughout the rest of my life. Who knew what was down the path I was about to set foot on?

I stood at a crossroads...with no idea where each way led. And with a pounding heart and cold fear in my throat, I prepared to make my choice.

Here's hoping the path wouldn't crumble beneath my feet and lead to a complete disaster...

Mia's story continues in *At Any Price...*.

ABOUT THE AUTHOR

Brenna Aubrey is a USA TODAY Bestselling Author of contemporary romance stories that center on geek culture.

She has always sought comfort in good books and the long, involved stories she weaves in her head. Brenna is a city girl with a nature-lover's heart. She therefore finds herself out in green open spaces any chance she can get. She's also a mom, teacher, geek girl, Francophile, unabashed video-game addict & eBook hoarder.

She currently resides on the west coast of the US with her husband, two children, and two adorable golden retrievers.